"Is that the way you spoke to Marcella?"

Raine's voice was angry. "Giving orders as if you were some sort of god?"

His black eyes kindled, though his voice was calm. "Leave Marcella out of it. You have taken her place, but that doesn't mean our relationship must follow the pattern that hers and mine did. We are us; we'll think and act as our own wills lead us."

Raine's brows shot up. "Have I any free will of my own, Darius?"

"You come to me of your own free will." He looked straight at her, challenge in his eyes. "How you love to deceive yourself, Raine. I once told you that I attract you as much as you attract me. You're fooling neither of us by pretending you dislike my lovemaking...."

ANNE HAMPSON

bitter harvest

Harlequin Books

TORONTO · LONDON · LOS ANGELES · AMSTERDAM
SYDNEY · HAMBURG · PARIS · STOCKHOLM · ATHENS · TOKYO

Harlequin Presents edition published January 1982
ISBN 0-373-10476-6

Original hardcover edition published in 1977
by Mills & Boon Limited

CHAPTER ONE

RAINE HANSFORD stood before the long, gilt-framed mirror and surveyed herself through critical eyes, eyes of deepest brown, set wide apart below a high unlined forehead. The white dress she wore was a model, long and flowing, with a high neckline and exceptionally wide sleeves gathered into tight cuffs at her wrists. Her long black hair fell with enchanting contrast on to her shoulders, and she smiled faintly at the effect. She turned from the waist, and her proud head lifted. No wonder, she thought, that no less than an earl had chosen her for his bride; she would make an exceptionally charming lady of quality.

Stephen ... A sigh escaped her and for a fleeting moment she thought of her sister, Drena, who had never ever intended marrying for anything but love. Love! Raine had been in love once, and met with disillusionment when her fiancé had been seen with another girl. He had been asked to do a week-end job on his friend's boat, he had told Raine, who, though bitterly disappointed that she and he would not be spending the week-end together, had to agree that the money he earned would come in handy in buying things for the home they were getting together.

He *had* been spending the week-end on the boat, yes, but with an old flame of his.

'What of it?' he had frowned when Raine, having been told of the escapade, had tackled him with it. 'No one ever bothers these days. I'll not do it when we're married, my pet!'

And so Raine had determined to marry for money—when eventually she did marry, that was. For after the break with her fiancé she had been a long time on her own, not desiring the company of the opposite sex. But then had come along Stephen, whom she had met by chance when paying an afternoon visit to the gymkhana which was being held in the village near his home. She had slipped on the damp grass and he had caught her before she fell. They had both laughed, then chatted, then gone over to the marquee and had tea together.

The courtship had been a whirlwind one, with Stephen—she suspected—feeling inordinately proud of her beauty, and she deciding that money, a title and a stately home would compensate very well for what she had suffered.

'Is he really in love with you?' Drena had asked doubtfully.

'I have no idea.'

'But—oh, Raine, don't do it! You're bitter over what you've suffered, but this isn't the answer. Neither of you *act* as if you're in love!'

Raine had shrugged. Not for her a second heartbreak, or period of humiliation when people offered their condolences. No, indeed not! Marry for money and rid oneself of the risk of disillusionment.

Another glance in the mirror revealed a lock of hair out of place; she picked up the comb and used it with care. Her face was rather pale, like alabaster, her lips full and parted slightly. She was extremely satisfied with herself this evening, since she was to receive the beautiful, flawless diamond which was a family heirloom and which Stephen had had altered slightly to fit her slender finger.

The engagement party was being held at Redmayne

6

House, Stephen's home, and all the nobility for miles around were invited, with others besides. Drena and her husband were to be there, but Drena was not in any way enthusiastic about the party.

'I feel you're putting your head in a noose,' she had said bluntly. 'I wish something would happen to stop the marriage.'

'It won't,' was Raine's confident rejoinder. 'Stephen wanted someone of whom he could be proud—a show-piece, of sorts—while I desire nothing more than the good life, with servants around me and clothes and jewels in plenty.'

'How bitter you are, and cynical!'

'Realistic, my dear sister.'

'It's not like you——'

'It must be; otherwise I wouldn't be doing it.'

'I believe you're determined to be hard.'

'Undoubtedly I'm determined to be hard. No man will ever hurt me again. Once I'm married to Stephen I shall be safe!'

'Supposing you fall in love, after you're married?'

'Not a hope,' returned Raine confidently. 'Once was more than enough for me.'

Raine was dancing with her fiancé when he sauntered in—the tall Greek with jet black hair and eyes that seemed equally dark. More distinguished-looking than any other man present, he stood for a moment, his eyes wandering round the brilliantly lighted room. Raine saw him at the same moment that he saw her; their eyes met, and held. She felt a strange tingling sensation run along her spine before, dragging her gaze from his, she turned to smile up at Stephen.

'Enjoying yourself?' he asked, and she nodded her head.

'Of course. It's marvellous!'

'A foretaste of things to come,' he said. 'Your life is shortly to undergo a most dramatic change.'

'I shall be Lady Redmayne.'

'My beautiful countess.'

Countess ... Her proud head lifted ... and once again her eyes met those of the Greek. He had never moved from his place by the high, arched opening which led from the hall to the ballroom.

'Who's the late arrival?' she inquired at last, and Stephen turned his head.

'Ah, it's Darius Kallergis from Delphi, in Greece! He's over here on a visit to his sister, who's married to an English businessman. Darius is a friend of my cousin John.'

Raine looked for John, saw his attention had already become focused on his friend. The two men gestured to one another; the next time Raine saw them was when, the dance finished, she was being introduced to the Greek.

'How do you do?' Her hand was taken in a firm grip that caused her to wince; her eyes were sought and held with a look so forceful and compelling that she found herself becoming vitally aware of his magnetism ... and his masculinity. He seemed to draw her and she knew a sort of helplessness which angered her.

'The glowing bride-to-be, eh?' Sarcasm edged his tone, and amusement, neither of which did he trouble to disguise.

Raine coloured, felt her fiancé's head lift, saw the surprise in John's blue eyes.

'How long are you here for?' inquired Stephen, his voice cold and unfriendly.

'Another week, that's all.'

'Have you had a pleasant time up till now?'

'Very, thank you.' The Greek made a little bow as he spoke, his black eyes fixed on Raine's face the whole time. Her colour heightened; it was a tense and uncomfortable moment, with no one offering to add to the stilted politeness of these words.

'Come,' said John awkwardly at length, 'I'll introduce you to my parents.'

It was less than ten minutes later when Raine, having been left for a few moments while Stephen danced with his mother, found herself looking up into the inscrutable mask of the Greek's face. She noted the classical features, the strong determined chin and firm, implacable jaw. His mouth was equally firm, but sensuous, for all that.

'Shall we dance?' he asked suavely, but afforded her no chance of refusing as, taking her hand, he drew her close to his body and swung her deftly on to the floor. She looked up, her heartbeats racing as the blood rushed through her veins. Every nerve seemed to be quivering, every pulse affected in some strange and frightening way. Within seconds she found herself being propelled towards the wide open window, outside of which was the verandah.

'Where——? I don't want to go out there!' she protested, but to no avail. 'How dare you force me out here?' She twisted from his arms and faced him, her cheeks pale with anger. 'We'll go back—at once!'

His hand shot out and she was literally dragged along the verandah, into darkness.

'A kiss, my beauty! What do you mean by becoming engaged to a colourless freak like Stephen Redmayne?'

She tried to push him away, but a little triumphant laugh escaped him at her helplessness as, bringing her against him, he crushed her within his arms and bent

9

his head to kiss her lips. She tried to struggle, then, exhausted, gave up.

'You—you—despicable cad!' she cried in a voice of white-hot fury when at last he released her. 'I shall go in there and denounce you to my fiancé!'

'I think not, my lovely Raine——'

'I'm not your Raine! Don't you dare to use my Christian name again!' She was attempting to move, but he had her prisoner against the wide marble pillar against which he had pushed her. His arms were outstretched at either side of her, his hands flat upon the pillar. 'Get away from me! I shall scream if you don't release me at once!'

'Scream away, my dear. I shall tell them you tempted me to bring you out here——'

'You wouldn't!' she cried disbelievingly, but he was slowly shaking his head and she added nothing to these two brief words of protest.

'I'd do just that, my lovely. I wanted to taste these beautiful lips the moment I set eyes on them—from across the width of that ballroom. And when John told me that you were the girl whose engagement party it was, I became keenly interested in the lucky man— and, my God, when I did see him I wondered what had possessed you to get yourself tied up with an insignificant whelp like that! You were meant for love; he can never give it to you. You were made for some man who could transport you to the very heights of——'

'Stop it!' Stooping swiftly, Raine hoped to slip beneath the circle of his arms, but he was too quick for her. She was caught in a primitive embrace that left her gasping; her face was jerked up by arrogant fingers, and her mouth crushed under his merciless, all-demanding lips. She swayed as his arms slackened, then was brought close again. His mouth was on hers, forcing her own bruised lips apart. She surrendered, both her lips and her body, and his hand came slowly, tantalisingly, from her slender hip to her waist and then his long lean fingers drew a line over the tender curve of her breast before his hand closed upon it, arrogantly, possessively. It was only when he would have slipped his hand beneath her shoulder strap, with the intention of dropping it, that she began to put up a determined and violent fight. She let out with her foot, catching him on the shin so that the gasp he gave was audible, affording her at least some satisfaction. But she was exhausted, had been even before she began to fight him, and a low laugh escaped him as her struggles began to ease off, then cease altogether.

She was crying, more with temper than anything else, but to herself she had to own that she was affected emotionally in a way she had never known existed. The man's whole strength had descended upon her, his magnetism held her, his dominance conquered the urge to do battle against him. She was ashamed to find herself comparing his lovemaking with that of Stephen's insipid kisses and his embrace. She was disgusted to find herself visualising the more passionate side of her marriage ... and to her amazement seeing this amorous Greek in the place of her husband!

'Another kiss, my beautiful Raine, and then we must return to the hall ...' His voice was vibrant at first, then it sank to a husky bass note as his lips moved closer to hers. She felt his warm clean breath on her face, quivered and trembled at the nearness of him, and as the blood raced through her she became enveloped in a tide of excitement that swept her to a state of half-fearful expectancy and, propelled by this vague force, she lifted her lips eagerly, surrendering them to the masterful demand of his.

A low laugh escaped him when eventually he held her at arms' length.

'You're trembling, my love——'

'I'm not your love, nor am I trembling!'

'You're trembling,' he repeated softly, bringing his cheek to hers. 'The result of nervous excitement and pleasure. We cannot stay out much longer ... but what about tomorrow night? Tell me where you live, and I'll call for you in my hired car——'

'Don't be ridiculous!' She tried to wrench herself free, but his arm caught her to him, roughly and ruthlessly.

'You try my patience, Raine,' he told her sternly. 'I fail to understand your attitude when, quite willingly, you've responded to my kisses.'

'Willingly? No such thing! Let me go this minute or, I warn you, I *shall* call out!'

'Call away, my dear,' he challenged softly. 'You're going to look pretty foolish, all dishevelled and red in the face, quivering with suppressed passion——'

'Shut up!' she snapped, a surge of embarrassment and humiliation enveloping her. 'What a despicable cad you are! Is this the way you treat every woman you meet?'

'Indeed no.' His cheek was against hers again. 'But you—you, my beauty, drew me as no other woman has ever drawn me before—oh, I've had affairs, several, but never have I felt like this. I want you, Raine ... and I shall have you, no matter how you feel at this moment. Once you're alone, perhaps in your bedroom tonight, you will think of my kisses ... and want more than kisses. I shall leave you my telephone number, and you'll ring me to make a date.'

She was silent for a space. Her mind had been rehearsing what she would say, the idea having soared into her brain while he was speaking.

'I hate to—to admit it,' she said jerkily, 'but—but you are right. I d-did respond willingly to your kisses, and —and I know already that—that I w-want more than kisses from you.' For effect she buried her face in his coat. 'What have you done to me?'

'Shown you what love can be!' was his vibrant and triumphant reply. 'My love! You are going to meet me tomorrow night?'

'That's what I was going to say. Give me your telephone number and I'll ring you.' A small pause, also for effect. 'I feel so ashamed——'

'Then don't! Life is for living—and you and I shall live it. You can't marry this man now. You know it, don't you?'

Raine nodded, but said no word. She had achieved her desire—that he would not pester her any further tonight. The acceptance of his telephone number would satisfy him that he was going to get all he wanted from her. Arrogant, self-opinionated ass! Did he really think he could force her to suffer his lovemaking? She had heard all about the amorous nature of the Greeks, knew they called their lovers 'pillow friends'. She was aware of their inflated ego where conquests were concerned—but if this Darius Kallergis thought that he had made a conquest tonight, then he was in for a disappointment!

'I must go in,' she said presently. 'I'll be missed.'

'Unfortunately, yes.' His arms were around her, their strength infallible. And so she stood motionless while the silence between them stretched, as if to eternity. The clouds had parted and a misted moon appeared from between them. In its calm light all was silvered; Raine could see the dim outline of Darius's face, hard, like granite. He looked into her eyes and she swiftly lowered her lashes, unwilling to let him see her expression, even though she doubted his ability to read it, standing in the shadows as they were.

She remained motionless, and the silence became an interlude of expectancy. She tried to force some action into her unresisting body, but she seemed totally under the influence of his domination as, sweeping her into an embrace that was as passionate as it was arrogant, he pressed his hard demanding mouth to hers.

'You're mine!' he told her ardently when at last she was free. 'Heaven is just a few hours away!'

At last they turned into the light and walked along the verandah towards the ballroom window. Raine felt utterly weak and helpless, with every nerve in her body tensed, every sense vitally stirred by the dramatic scene in which she had taken part. It seemed unreal, a dream which had left her dazed and shaken, but a dream for all that.

'Where have you two been?' It was Stephen's mother who asked the question as they stepped from the verandah into the ballroom. She looked from one to the other, her narrowed eyes dark and suspicious. 'Raine, your hair's—er— rather awry, to say the least.'

'The breeze, madam,' interposed Darius with swift assurance. 'Miss Hansford was rather warm and I suggested I take her on to the verandah where she could have the soft breeze fan her face.' He was all suave ease and politeness, his handsome face a mask of untroubled calm. Raine, on the other hand, was having the greatest difficulty in concealing the nervous tension within her. Her hands trembled and she closed them tightly; her lips had also to be shut tightly as otherwise their quivering would have been uncontrollable.

'Oh, I see.' But Raine did not think for one moment

14

that her future mother-in-law did see. Her expression was one of frowning puzzlement, and her examination of Raine's flushed face was hard and intense. This was not the first time that Raine had been starkly reminded that Stephen's parents had not welcomed their son's decision to marry so far beneath him. 'Well, I should go and find Stephen, if I were you! He's been looking around for you for the past quarter of an hour.' And with this she turned away, her tall aristocratic figure carried with well-bred ease of movement, so that she appeared to be gliding rather than walking with her feet upon the floor.

'Are you intending to have *that* criticising your every action all your life?' he asked with a sort of lazy amusement.

'She had every right to ask me where I'd been!'

He shook his head.

'No human being has the right to question the actions of another. We are each entitled to a free life.'

She was swift to take him up on this.

'If you had a wife, would you question her actions?'

A strange expression entered his black eyes; they seemed to open wide, then narrow a little.

'That,' he said at last, 'is a very different matter indeed.'

She looked at him with a hint of contempt.

'Avoiding the issue, are you?'

'A husband's role is very different from that of a woman who is not yet even your mother-in-law. And she never will be your mother-in-law,' he added, rather quickly, and in a softer tone, for out of the corner of his eye he saw Raine's fiancé approaching. Suavely he swung round to face him: 'Your charming fiancée has done me the honour of giving me a few minutes of her company. I hand her safely back to you.'

15

Stephen's face darkened at the bland manner in which the Greek spoke to him. But, remembering his good manners just in time, he forced a smile and said,

'Thank you, Mr Kallergis. Raine, my dear, let me take you over to the refreshment table.'

His mother joined them, and Raine suspected this was deliberate even before she said,

'Raine, you didn't tidy your hair—after being outside with that foreigner. I should do so at once if I were you.'

'You were outside with him?' Stephen looked darkly at his fiancée.

Raine had coloured hotly, and now her head was bent. She was overwhelmed with guilt, and furiously angry because of it. That hateful creature, to subject her to embarrassment such as this!

'It was rather warm, and he suggested we went on to the verandah, to cool off.'

'A most strange suggestion for a man to make to his host's fiancée.' Stephen's mother had adopted a haughty manner, and a denunciatory one. 'I hope it won't happen again.'

Raine's head came up, and a retort leapt to her lips. But she held it back, for there was too much at stake. She wanted more than anything to marry Stephen—merely because he represented the money for which she had vowed to marry—and she was not willing to risk anything going wrong at this stage of her game.

'It won't,' she returned, adopting a meekness which only added to the anger within her. 'I suppose it was the wrong thing to do, but I never gave it a thought at the time.'

The older woman nodded, appearing to be mollified. Stephen was eating, and his eyes were wandering around; she wondered if his eyes sought the tall Greek, who seemed to have disappeared.

However, he reappeared the moment Raine was alone again. This happened when Stephen, approached unashamedly by one of his old flames who chided him for neglecting to dance with her, went off after making a brief apology to Raine. She had found a chair in a little alcove, but, seeing Darius making his way determinedly through the throng of dancers, rose swiftly and, in a sort of panic, decided to hide herself in the small sitting-room which was used by the family only, and mainly by Stephen's parents. In order to reach this apartment she had to leave the alcove by a small door, traverse a corridor, cross the secondary hallway, and then mount a small, thickly-carpeted staircase. Once in the room she closed the door and, sinking into a chair, breathed freely again. One table lamp was all that lit the room; it was very dim, with an amber-coloured shade. It was a restful light and she savoured the peace around her. No sound here; not even the strains of the dance music had penetrated the distance from the massive banqueting hall where the party was being held.

Suddenly she froze, without knowing why. No sound caught her ears, but she felt she should have heard one. Then, before her fascinated gaze, the door handle moved, followed by the noiseless opening of the door itself.

Her heart sank. She knew even before she saw the dim outline of the tall Greek, that it was he who would enter the room.

'Get out!' she seethed, rising to her feet. 'I came in here for a little peace!'

'To collect yourself?' He seemed to give this a second's thought before adding, in that lazy languid drawl which she had heard before, 'Perhaps it was to collect yourself, but mainly, it was with the intention of escaping me. I followed you, Raine, as I will always follow you if ever you try to elude me. I want you, and it is my intention to have you.'

She was on her feet, facing him in anger. His eyes flickered, caressing her beautiful face and her neck and the curve of her breasts before travelling to her tiny waist and slender hips. She felt she was being stripped naked; she knew his desire was so high that, had the situation allowed it, he would without doubt have attempted to take her, to conquer and possess her. The idea was terrifying while at the same time unquestionably exciting. What had this pagan done to her? Why was it that although her chief emotion was that of fury, there ran alongside this a strange unfathomable yearning, a vague desire, an unexpectancy that in itself bred fear?

'Please go,' she ordered, but without revealing her anger. 'I've promised to phone you and make a date——'

'It struck me,' he broke in, 'that you might not have meant what you said, that you had made the promise under stress and that you had no intention of keeping it. I therefore desired to speak with you again, and to warn you that I make no idle small talk when I say that I shall have you——'

'Not small talk, no! Just rubbish!' This was out before she realised what she had admitted, but Darius brought it to her mind by saying, his voice crisp, his black eyes narrowed to mere slits,

'So you never did intend to keep your word? I was correct in my suspicions.' His mouth twisted and Raine thought she had never seen so evil an expression in the whole of her life. 'Cheat! And now, my girl, you'll pay!' He crossed the room with lightning speed; she was in his arms before she knew it and his mouth, forcing her lips open, demanded her reciprocation to his kisses. For an eternity she held out, while he drew her quivering body to his with what she could only describe as primitive passion. She surrendered at last, her own desire fanned to a flame by his arrogant mastery of her. Her thoughts gave out and she was wandering in a fog, with only caution to restrain her from exquisite and total submission.

'Let me go,' she pleaded when eventually she was allowed to speak. 'I want to return to my fiancé.'

'Liar ...' So soft the voice, and confident. His strong arms encased her slim young body, a pliant, yielding body that protested against the restraint which she was attempting valiantly to put upon it. But she felt defenceless, and when he once more bent to kiss her she lifted her head a little higher, submissively offering him her lips. 'Yes ... liar,' he breathed as he drew his mouth from hers. 'You have not the least desire to go to your fiancé. For you are finding me as irresistible as I find you——No,' he said imperiously when she would have interrupted him, 'do not deny it, my beautiful Raine! Desire is in your eyes and in your heart. You'd surrender at this moment were we not here, in this house. But tomorrow night, my love ... you will come to a small hotel I know of. It's by a swiftly-flowing river—right on the bank, as a matter of fact—and there, with that lovely sound in our ears, we shall make love. You'll be taken to heaven over and over again——'

'Be quiet!' she seethed, able to interrupt at last. 'You talk as if we've known each other for a long while! We're strangers! Do you hear me—strangers!'

'I do hear you, my love—and so will everyone else, if you raise your voice like this.'

'I can't help it! Oh, please let me go!'

'Why should I? We're both enjoying it, here in this private little room, with the most romantic golden light enhancing your beauty—Do you know that you have the classical features of a lovely Greek *koré*?' He traced a line from her high wide forehead to her firm but adorably feminine chin. 'Kiss me,' he commanded softly. And, when she took no notice, 'I said—kiss me!' His tone was an order, the order of a lord to his vassal. Raine suddenly found herself imbued with the strength to retaliate and, twisting out of his embrace, she stood with her back to the door, her eyes flashing with anger.

'You—egotistical, pompous ass! Who do you think you are that you can treat me like one of your subjugated Greek women! How dare you order me to——'

'I shall not order, then,' he broke in with suave arrogance. 'I shall just take.' And he began to advance towards her across the small apartment. She took a backward step which brought the door handle into touching distance. Darius smiled quizzically and shook his head. 'There's no escape, my love,' he assured her, but stopped in his tracks. She knew instinctively that he wanted her to make an endeavour to escape, just for the satisfaction of mastering her by preventing her from doing so. She made no move, but stood motionless, her face white, her hands closed so tightly that perspiration was gathering in her palms. Her whole body trembled, while her mind rebelled at this position in which she found herself. It seemed impossible that it was real, incredible that she had not been able to control it, that, on the contrary, she had remained almost passive while he—this pagan from the East whom she had never even met a couple of hours ago—had exerted his will upon her, forcing her reciprocation against all her determination and reluctance. The power of him was unbelievable; he possessed a mastery and dominance which she seemed quite unable to combat.

'Yes,' he was saying into her thoughts, 'I shall take ... always, Raine. Get that into your lovely head. I take what I want, and I want you.'

She shook her head vigorously, tears of frustration starting to her eyes as she watched him cover the distance between them with no more than a couple of long and easy strides. She was taken into his arms and brought to his lean lithe body. Her head was lifted by his hand under her chin. His black eyes regarded her with sardonic amusement, while the half-smile hovering on his thin lips taunted even while it betrayed the triumph within him. It faded as his lips met hers; she stood against him, defeated by the strength of him, both physically and mentally. She was vitally aware of his hard body, of the wild beating of his heart which seemed as rapid as her own. After a while she was pulled into the middle of the room; she saw that his intention was to take possession of the couch and she recoiled instantly. But she was not allowed to break away. Instead, she was arrogantly swung back into his arms and her lips, already swollen and bruised, were even yet again subjected to his mastery.

Then suddenly there was an alertness about him, and Raine wondered afterwards if it were only she herself who was startled by the opening of the door behind her, wondered if Darius could have eased the situation by a rapid movement to the other side of the room.

'So ...' The voice of Stephen's mother was like the sound of metal scraping on rock. 'I wasn't mistaken when I thought you'd been up to something, out there on the verandah! Stephen———!' She turned to the young man standing just behind her. 'Perhaps you will now begin to understand why your father and I had no desire to have this woman as our daughter-in-law!'

'But it isn't wh-what it s-seems——' began Raine in disjointed accents, only now aware that she had failed to wrench herself from Darius's arms. She had been frozen into immobility by the unexpected appearance of Stephen and his mother, and all she knew was that a torrent of self-criticism was flooding over her.

'Not what it seems?' repeated Stephen, his eyes dark with contempt as he watched Raine disengage herself and stand, a few paces from the tall, unperturbed Greek, her hands twisting and untwisting as her nervous embarrassment was revealed. 'I don't think I understand, Raine?'

She heard the acid tone of his voice, saw the triumphant expression on his mother's lined and haughty face . . . and she knew that all her scheming had come to nought, destroyed by this calm and smiling Greek whose eyes were fixed upon the man in whose house he was a guest.

CHAPTER TWO

RAINE had been pacing her room for over an hour, brooding on what she had lost—and through no fault of her own ... Or was it? Surely she could have held the creature off? Surely she could have prevented him from taking her on to the verandah in the first place, and then following her to the small sitting-room afterwards? She should have had the sense to glance back as she made her way from the alcove to the small apartment. Strangely, it had never entered her head, at the time, that he would follow her. Yet now it seemed that it was the kind of thing he most certainly would do.

'I could kill him!' she fumed, glancing at the third finger of her left hand. For a few hours she had worn the expensive diamond, then had been ordered by Stephen to hand it back to him. His mother had taken it from him, she recalled, and slipped it on to her own finger.

Then came that ignominious moment when she and Darius Kallergis had been ordered from the house, the lovely stately home of which she had believed she would one day become mistress. Darius had been amused by the whole episode, telling her that it had made things simple for her, as she was not now faced with the unpleasant task of telling Stephen that she herself was breaking the engagement. He was driving her home at the time, in the car he had hired for the duration of his stay in England.

'Why so glum, my beauty? Our path has been

smoothed for us and you should be feeling exceedingly happy about it.'

'Happy?' she flared, half turning her head to give him a vicious glance. 'Do you realise what I've lost?'

'Materially?' was his smooth inquiry, 'or emotionally?'

'I love him!' she snapped.

'You lie far too easily, Raine. I fear I shall have to chastise you about it.' The road was a silver stream of moonlight stretching before them; his hands on the wheel were relaxed and his voice was calm, tinged with mocking humour that yet held an edge of sternness, and warning. Raine seethed but said nothing. All she desired was to get home, to find herself alone in her room, where she could give vent to her feelings either by tears or bitter invective against this pagan who had, within the period of a few hours, wrecked her whole life, completely destroying her chance of becoming the wife of the man who could have given her both wealth and a title.

On reaching home he had stopped the car, then possessively taken her in his arms and kissed her. Raine had offered no resistance, deciding it were better to let him take what he wanted and be gone.

'I could kill him!' she repeated, still pacing the bedroom. 'Why has he done this to me—me! He could have found a dozen women there this evening who would have been only to willing to have succumbed to his desires!' Yes, Raine was under no illusions as to the private lives of 'Our Betters'. Those whose lives were lived in idleness would always find an outlet for their energies and emotions. And the affairs that went on among Stephen's set had at first appalled her, but she had gradually accepted them, at the same time vaguely wondering if she herself would ever seek distraction in a

24

similar way. She knew for sure that Stephen would be unfaithful, probably over and over again, but she did not care. She was interested in his wealth and his title, not the man himself. She had never liked his father, the Marquis, and she had disliked his mother even more. It had given her a high degree of satisfaction to know that they would have preferred their son to have chosen a girl of the nobility; she was human enough to gloat secretly at their disappointment in having a commoner enter the august portals of Redmayne House.

And now it was their turn to gloat, to tell their son that he had had a narrow escape.

At last Raine took a bath—for a warm bath always had had a most sobering effect on her—and got into bed. Lying there, wide awake, she naturally recalled what the Greek had said to her. She would think of his kisses ... and want more than kisses. Conceited pagan that he was! Well, he would soon know whether she wanted more or not! A sneer curved her mouth as she reflected on his passing her a piece of paper on which was written his telephone number. If she should fail to ring him, he had warned, then he would not hesitate to call her at home and demand to see her.

She would not be here. As yet she did not know what she intended doing, but she did know that she was never going to see that man ever again. She happened to be just starting a week's holiday, her boss having decided she ought to be compensated for the many hours of overtime she had put in over the past year. So she could go away, miles away, and the Greek would have left England by the time she returned.

She continued to lie awake, filled with dejection at the loss she had sustained. She had gone out this evening in the highest of spirits, filled with elation that she should be wearing her ring in a very short time, a ring which spelt security, and all the good things of life. Her broken romance had faded from her mind; it no longer hurt to think that her fiancé had been unfaithful, had lightly taken a week-end with another girl. Let him have her! She, Raine, had come off best, after all.

But it was no such thing now. Through the mischief wrought by that dark foreigner whom she hated with a black venom, her bright future had become blotted out by clouds.

At four o'clock she was still awake. The sun was still obscured, but its light hovered in the eastern sky, pearl-grey and soft. The first bird sent its trill across the garden, then another song was heard, and another, until it seemed that the whole wide world was echoing with music. Raine rose and, going over to the window, opened the curtains to their full extent, widening the view she had had when lying in bed. A brooding lone-liness hung over the garden, which extended to a line of poplar trees beyond which could be seen the softly-curving lines of a range of low hills. Raine had a flat in this dignified Georgian house, and in it were a few lovely antiques rescued when, on the death of her parents, everything they owned had to be sold to pay the debts which, unknown to their daughters, they had been running up for years. Drena had protested that they were not getting full value for what was being sold, and it was her idea that she and Raine should take out one or two special pieces and say nothing about them. It was dishonest, Raine had pointed out, but Drena would not agree. And so Raine had taken a rosewood sideboard and two armchairs, also one or two choice pieces of porcelain. The bedroom furniture had also been 'rescued', as Drena insisted on terming it, and the two girls had each taken a full suite.

'There's oceans of stuff left,' Drena had pointed out. 'Why should you, who have nothing with which to furnish the flat you've taken, be reduced to buying rubbish on the never-never? And why should I, who am just married and getting a home together, also buy rubbish? No, let's take a few of the best pieces. In any case, we do need something to remember our parents by.'

Raine had said nothing. She and Drena had never been close to their parents. On the contrary, they had been pushed out of their affections at very early ages, and had they not had each other they would have been very lonely indeed. Their parents had died in an accident when the motor coach on which they were travelling across France had crashed. As was usual, they had taken the holiday on their own, not even having asked if their children would like to accompany them.

Raine gave a small sigh and dismissed these memories from her mind. It was useless to brood on the fact that she and Drena had never known parental love. Their mother and father had needed no one but each other; they were sufficient unto themselves. They had died together and their daughters felt it was fate that this should be so, as neither would have lasted long without the other.

The morning bird-song was still ringing in her ears when at last Raine turned from the window. She reflected again on what had transpired the previous evening, admitting to her amazement that the dance with the Greek had been the most pleasant she had ever experienced. Her feet had seemed scarcely to touch the floor; her mind was profoundly conscious of his touch, of the warmth of his hand through the thin material of her dress, of his incredible height and his good looks ... of the envious glances of some of the 'set' who, Raine strongly suspected, were excitedly waiting for the Greek to change partners!

Then the interlude on the verandah, and the shock

which she received from his incredible conduct. That the whole situation savoured of the primitive was without question; he was a pagan and he revealed this by his arrogant assumption of authority over her. She would bow to his demands; it was as simple and untrammelled as that. She would give up her fiancé because he, Darius Kallergis, said so; she would then indulge in an affair with him. Yes, she had no other ideas as to the relationship which he had decided would develop between them. His pillow friend—or one of them—she would be, cast off when he became tired of her. It was unbelievable, and she did wonder what would be her sister's reaction if she should ever relate what had happened. As it was, Raine intended merely to inform Drena that she had changed her mind about marrying Stephen, a decision which would meet with Drena's complete approval.

Again Raine's thoughts went off at a tangent and she was re-living that momentous period which, although so brief, had changed her whole life. She could almost feel those savage, satanic kisses—but why not, seeing that her mouth was still bruised and swollen? She could feel his hands upon her, could live again through that sensation when, drawn by his magnetism, she had surrendered her lips ... and half-longed to surrender her body. Yes, it was futile to deny it; she had been tempted as she had never been tempted before ... and by a man whose strength left her feeling as weak as a baby.

What must she do? That he would come and seek her out she had no doubt at all. He obviously thought he would meet someone other than herself if he came to her house tomorrow night as he had threatened. He would probably expect to meet at least one of her parents, as she had not made any mention of being an orphan. Nor did he know she lived in a flat in this house. She supposed the logical thing to have done last night was to have refused his offer of a lift. But it was very late and there were no buses. Stephen quite naturally made no offer to take her home. Another switch of thought and she was reflecting on Drena's surprise when she discovered her sister had left the party. What Stephen would say Raine had no idea, but she felt sure he would not say anything about the scene in the small sitting-room. He would put Drena off with some story that her sister had been so tired that she had decided to go home. Drena did not get along with him; so it was reasonable to assume she would refrain from asking him too many questions.

'He's such a snob,' she had said so often. 'I hate even speaking to him.'

What must she do? Raine was again asking herself. She must not be here when that man arrived, that was for sure. She would sleep if she could, for then she would be able to think more clearly, and make a decision. With this in her mind she got back into bed, and although she lay awake for some time, unable to stop thinking of last night, the final thread of consciousness did eventually fade and she slept, not waking until noon.

The first thing that came to her mind as she opened her eyes was an offer made to her by a colleague who owned a caravan in Wales.

'If you ever want to take a nice restful holiday away from it all,' this girl had said, 'you can have my caravan. It's up in the hills, on a sheep farm belonging to my uncle—all wild country around, but the van's in a pretty little copse and you'll adore it!'

'I'll take her up on that,' decided Raine, jumping out of bed and picking up the phone. In less than five minutes her plans were made; she was to pick up the key, and the address, from her colleague at the office that very afternoon. What a fortunate circumstance it was that she happened to be off work. Today was Monday; she did not have to be back at the office until the following Monday, and by that time the Greek would have left the country. 'And may I never cross his path again!' she was saying fervently as she began to pack in readiness for the journey. 'Meeting him was the worst thing that ever happened in the whole of my life!'

By late evening she was settled in the caravan, having gone into Wales by train and then taken a taxi to the farm, where she was welcomed warmly by the owner, Mr Chesworth, who took her up to the caravan in his jeep, bringing water and a new bottle of butane gas.

He had left her quite soon, and she was relieved by this, having feared he might stay, her company being welcome in so remote a place.

'If you get tired of your own company,' he had smiled on getting into his jeep, 'come on down and have a chat with my wife and me.'

Raine thanked him, then set about unpacking her clothes and the food she had brought with her, most of which was in packets or tins—although she had bought a ready roasted chicken and it was of this, with some salad, that she made her first meal.

The meal over, she washed the dishes, then ventured out for a short walk, choosing the grassy slopes rather than the steep path along which she had been brought earlier. The region was lonely, with indistinct shapes moving about—sheep on the hillsides and the moors.

She walked for a while and then turned back, a deep sigh leaving her lips. So different this from last night, when, filled with hope for the future, she had set forth to her own engagement party. So much to happen in so short a time.

Reaching the caravan, she entered, and within a quarter of an hour she was in bed where, to her surprise, her mind immediately became hazy, and she fell into a restful, dreamless sleep. She awoke to the sun streaming through the uncurtained window which looked on to the woods. The air was fresh as it drifted through the fanlight above her head and she rose instantly, wondering why she was not feeling so depressed as she was yesterday. Then she realised that at least her fear had vanished, fear that the Greek would come to her home and pester her. Here, in this remote spot among the hills, she was safe . . . safe until he had left the country in less than a week's time, when she would be able to return to her home and take up life where she had left it off before she met Stephen.

It was late afternoon, three days later when, getting back from a long walk, Raine opened the door of the caravan, which she had not troubled to lock since there was not a living soul in the area, and stood, frozen into immobility, every vestige of colour leaving her face.

'Hello, Raine,' said that lazy, accented voice. 'You look more desirable than ever. The country air is obviously doing you good.'

'What——? How—how did you find m-me?' Her voice was strained, husky with fear. 'I—I can't th-think why you should w-want to come up—up here——?'

'To find you, my dear,' he interrupted suavely, rising from his most comfortable position on the settee by the open window. 'What a beautiful place you have here. It's much more secluded . . . and romantic than the little hotel by the river which I spoke of.' A pause and then, 'Come here, Raine.' So soft the voice, but commanding for all that. Raine turned swiftly and was through the door and down the steps in a matter of seconds. Hair flying, she raced along the path, with

Darius following, and swiftly catching her up. She took a bend, and saw his car, blocking her way. Sobbing and breathless, she swerved, into the marshy, uneven ground at the side of the path. Her foot caught in some kind of a root and, losing her balance, she fell headlong into the marsh, catching her head on the stump of a dead tree as she did so. A hundred points of light flashed through her brain before a great cloud blotted out her vision and blackness enveloped her completely.

She was in bed when she came round; with the blood surging into her face she realised she was naked beneath the covers. Tears stung her eyes as she looked up into the dark satanic features of the Greek.

'You—undressed m-me,' she said weakly, scarcely knowing what words left her quivering lips.

'Of course,' imperturbably as he took her hand to feel her pulse. 'The only sensible thing to do since your clothes were soaking wet.'

She swallowed, feeling faint and dreadfully weak and scared. Naked ... It was too terrifying for thought. Here she was, miles from any habitation except for the farm, which itself was at least half a mile away. What a fool she was to think he would never find her! She should have paid more attention to his threats, should have been more alertly on her guard.

'I've hurt my head,' she murmured, aware of his warm fingers pressed to her wrist.

'It isn't much, just a nasty cut which I've cleaned up and covered with a dressing I found in your first aid box in the cupboard over there.'

'Just a nasty cut ...?' Why wasn't it serious enough for him to be compelled to get a doctor, who would see that she was admitted to hospital? The tears trickled on to her cheeks; she noted his changing expression, saw the dark features relax, the mouth become more full, the black eyes soften a little.

'There's no need to cry,' he told her quietly. 'You're not badly hurt at all, just shaken, and perhaps a little weak?'

She nodded her head.

'I do feel weak,' she admitted, and made an attempt to sit up, making sure to keep the bedcovers held close to her throat. Darius gently put her back on the pillow.

'Stay there,' he said. 'I'll get you something to drink. What would you like? Something warm, like milk, or a drop of brandy?'

'There isn't any brandy.'

'There's a small bottle in the first aid box. Didn't you know?'

'It isn't my caravan,' she told him by way of explanation. And then she added, 'How did you find me?'

He smiled, his eyes crinkling with amusement.

'It was easy. You silly, misguided child. Why didn't you telephone me as I asked you to——'

'Ordered, you mean,' she interrupted, anger entering into her despite her feeling of fatigue.

'Ordered if you like,' he agreed imperturbably. 'To run away was a childish act, and a futile one, as you have now discovered. I said I would follow you, and I meant it.'

'You haven't told me how you managed to find me?'

'I called at your home on the evening you should have phoned me, and discovered it was a flat in which you lived. You'd gone away, the young woman in the upper flat informed me. A taxi had come for you and she saw you get into it, with a suitcase and a large box.'

Her clothes and her food. Susie, in the flat above, seemed to spend half her time at the window—looking out on to the park opposite, she would maintain.

'She didn't know where I was going, though.'

'I assumed you'd hire a taxi from the firm nearest to where you lived. I found the firm and learned that you'd been taken to the Farne Road station to catch a train for Dolgellau, in Wales.'

'So you immediately motored to Dolgellau,' she stated, and Darius nodded his head.

'Once there, I discovered that a young lady had arrived on that particular train and had hired a taxi to take her to Chesworth's Farm——'

'Did Mr Chesworth send you up here?' she gasped, unable to believe that he would do such a thing, with the caravan being in so lonely a place.

'I said I had an urgent message for you,' answered Darius calmly. 'I must have impressed Mrs Chesworth —I did not see her husband—as being both respectable and sincere.' Raine said nothing; she was mystified by his persistence, as all this must surely have interfered drastically with the plans he had made for his visit to England. However, as her chief and most vital action at the moment must be to escape, she determinedly switched her thoughts to devising some means whereby she could effect that escape.

And as the only thing she could think of was to pretend to be very ill, she gave a little groan, turned on her side, and began to breathe heavily.

'Raine!' The voice had lost its calm edge and seemed to have taken on a tinge of anxiety. 'What is it? Are you in pain?'

'Yes ... oh, *yes*!'

Silence. She knew without any doubt at all that she had erred, and by the vehemence with which she had spoken the last word. Her groan had been weak, but then she had suddenly spoken loudly, and strongly.

'My dear Raine,' came Darius's smooth voice at last, 'you'll have to try much harder than that if you want to deceive me. I'm expecting you to be perfectly all right by the morning.'

And she was. Immediately on waking she knew she had never felt better physically. But, mentally, she was in a state of high fever, with her thoughts flitting about in the most haphazard fashion possible. Her eyes went to the door of the bunk room at the far end of the caravan. It was closed. Last evening it had been wide open and she knew without any doubt at all that Darius had slept in there last night. She knew he was still there, since it was only half-past five, with the sun only just coming up over the hills. Escape! Slipping noiselessly from the bed, and wrapping herself in the sheet, she glanced around in an urgent search for her clothes. Had he given her something in that drink last evening? she wondered, silently opening a drawer to see if he had put her clothes in there. No, she did not believe he had given her anything, she was amazed to find herself deciding. From the first there had registered in her subconscious the fact that there was something good in him despite his brutal treatment of her. It amazed her to admit it, but she felt he had a certain code of honour which he would keep no matter what the circumstances.

It was all most illogical, she thought, opening another drawer and frowning, for it was empty. She had put blouses in there ... Suddenly she went rigid as suspicion dawned. Swiftly she went over to the wardrobe; it was the last place left. Empty! She had no clothes to put on, no shoes, nor even the mackintosh which she had hung on a hook right in the corner of the wardrobe.

Anger and despair brought the tears to her eyes. She might have known he'd make sure she could not escape him!

Her clothes and shoes were in the bunk room, where he was sleeping. Raine suddenly looked down at the sheet, her heart throbbing so swiftly and painfully that

35

she felt she must collapse if it continued like this. She could even hear it, hammering against her ribs.

'Oh, God, please help me!' Tears rolled down her cheeks and she lifted the sheet to wipe them away. The sheet ... Again she looked down at it, then suddenly made her decision. It would be embarrassing, and certainly not the way she would have wanted it, but she had no other option than to go down to the farm and seek help. 'I'll have to give them some sort of explanation,' she whispered silently. 'Oh, that a *stranger* should have brought me to an action like this!'

However, with her decision made she wasted no further time, and instantly made for the door. It was locked, and the key—which she had always left in the door—was missing.

White-hot fury blazed within her, thrusting out every other emotion. She would not let him beat her! The window could very soon be opened, and within seconds she was standing on a chair, ready to step through it.

'Going somewhere?' The suave and gentle voice might have been the crack of a rifle, such terror did it bring to her. Every nerve in her body tingled; her brain seemed affected also, for she felt a pounding sensation which threatened to deprive her of her senses. Darius, attired in a black dressing-gown trimmed with a very narrow edging of red on the collar and cuffs, looked, to her terrified imagination, like the devil himself. His black hair was awry; the overnight growth of his beard lent an added darkness to a face already burnt as brown as that of an Arab. Raine shivered but made a valiant effort to hold back the tears which fear was causing to form at the backs of her eyes. Automatically she clutched at the front of the sheet, as if she found protection in the act. Darius's lips were twitching, and his eyes were sending their amused glance from her face to her feet and back again. Anger ousted fear a little as she realised just how foolish she must look, standing on the chair in her bare feet, her body wrapped in a sheet. A retort leapt to her lips but was never uttered because Darius was speaking again.

'Allow me to help you down, my love. I wonder if I should spank you for trying to escape me like this? It's the second time, and if I'm to deter you from a further repetition I really do feel I must teach you a lesson——'

'Get away from me——' But already Darius had lifted her off the chair, and for a long moment he held her in his arms, staring down into her flushed face.

'By heaven, but you're a beauty!' His eyes darkened with ardour; she began to struggle and eventually was put down upon her feet. But any ideas she might have had of escaping that ardour were crushed on the instant, just as her lips were crushed beneath the merciless pressure of his.

'Let me go . . .' The plea was a silent one, for her lips were still captive beneath his. He forced her to reciprocate, just as he had done before. The tears escaped but had no effect upon him; his ardour had gone too far. He held her from him at last, and once again she started to struggle. He laughed and said in warning tones,

'You'll lose your protective covering if you're not careful, my love.'

Her struggles ceased and another laugh escaped him. 'Do you suppose I'm intending to allow you to retain that covering?' he queried smoothly, and already his hands were closed upon the sheet.

'Please . . .' Raine looked up into his unsmiling countenance. 'Can I appeal to anything that is good in you? What have I done that you want to treat me like this?' Her voice, low, and tinged with a sweetness never

37

heard since the breaking of her first engagement, carried a plea that would have melted a heart of stone. 'Let me go, I beg of you. There are plenty of women whom you can have——'

'But none like you,' he cut in vibrantly, and her heart sank with despair. 'The moment I saw you I became obsessed with the desire to taste your kisses; from there I wanted *you*!—wanted to sample an ambrosia I had never sampled before. It's no use your trying to escape fate, Raine. You and I were meant to meet, and to love. Nothing you can do will ever change what fate has planned for us.'

'You talk in the most absurd way.' Her voice was still low; she had noticed that his hands were no longer ready to strip the sheet from her, and she cherished the hope that she still might be able to escape the actual fire of his passion. 'We met quite by accident. Had you not been in England when my engagement was being celebrated then we'd never have met.'

'We did meet,' was his implacable rejoinder. 'I *was* in England when your engagement was being celebrated. It was fate, as I've said, and we must go where fate carries us—go together!'

He was tilting up her chin; in despair she saw the fire in his eyes being fanned to a flame. His hard demanding mouth took hers in arrogant possession and she had no strength left to fight him. She was so small in his arms, so helpless against his strength, so vulnerable to his masculine enticement.

'Give in,' he ordered, but gently. 'Your lips surrender, but your lovely body resists. You might as well resign yourself to the inevitable, my dear, and take what is your fate.'

'It will not be with desire on my part!' she flared. 'Resignation, yes! But you won't derive much satisfaction from making love to a block of ice!'

At this he held her from him, and laughed in sheer amusement. Raine saw the black eyes twinkle, their expression a supplement to his laughter.

'Bravado, my dear, and I'm surprised at you. Already you've given with these sweet lips; and, deep in this wildly-beating heart of yours, you know you'll allow yourself to be carried to the heights of ecstasy and bliss.'

She was hot and now even more colour rushed into her cheeks. For his hand was on her heart ... and she had not the strength or the desire to make any attempt to remove it.

She felt him stoop a little, to lift her off her feet. She was aware of the sheet becoming loosened by his action, and knew that part of it was draped against his legs. The bed was at the end of the caravan and he moved towards it with rhythmic steps. No use to struggle any more, she thought, trying to shut out the scene which was soon to be enacted, the scene when, tempted by his overwhelming magnetism and power, she would surrender, just as he had declared she would.

'There.' He had laid her on the bed, but stood looking down into her eyes. 'How did I come to find someone as lovely as you, my Raine?' His long lean fingers were fumbling a little as he untied the cord of his dressing-gown. The top part above the waist came open; she saw a mass of thick black hair among which was a small gold crucifix which hung from a fine gold chain. Sickened by what she considered to be the sheer hypocrisy of the man, she turned her head away, burying it in the pillow.

CHAPTER THREE

'So you turn from me, eh?' His voice, vibrant with passion, was yet amused as well, and almost instantly a low laugh was issuing from his lips. 'What an exciting little wretch you are! Subduing you will be made all the more pleasurable by this attitude you're adopting——' Suddenly, abruptly, his voice cut. 'What was that?'

Raine had heard it too, the cry of a ewe in distress. Following on almost immediately came another sound, that of a sheepdog snarling.

She sat up, holding the sheet in front of her. Darius, she saw as she turned her head, was already at the window in the little kitchen which went off the main living-room of the caravan. Through the open door she watched him open the curtains just sufficiently for him to see through, into the garden and the copse beyond.

He turned at last, the hint of a smile in his eyes.

'I do believe you're saved,' he murmured on a sardonic note. 'But I warn you, my love, it'll only be a temporary reprieve ...' His voice faded and he moved towards the bed, and stood for a long moment, observing her with an inscrutable expression in his dark and faintly narrowed eyes. 'So ...' he said at last, and the smile in his eyes reappeared, reflecting the amusement portrayed in his voice, 'you're not all joy at your escape——'

'Don't be ridiculous! Of course I'm all joy! I want to shout out with relief!'

But ... did she? Stunned by the question which had

intruded like a flash into her mind, she gave a little inward gasp. And then, desiring only to get away from the maelstrom of these disturbing sensations, she asked what was happening outside. She also asked about Darius's car and was told it was in a little copse, well hidden from the eyes of the farmer.

'As to what's happening out there,' continued Darius, 'the farmer appears to be coming here.' He looked at her and actually grinned. 'That's why I said you'd escaped.' Raine said nothing; she was recalling that, yesterday morning, a fox had come to attack a lamb and Mr Chesworth, warned by the cry, had raced up the hillside with his dog. 'Here's your housecoat.' Darius had been to the bunk room and brought forth the dainty garment. 'I took all your clothes,' he said with a faint smile, 'and I locked the door and withdrew the key. I didn't expect you to attempt an escape by the window, I must admit. An oversight which I must not allow to happen again.' He was watching her as she manoeuvred—while sitting up in bed—to get herself in the housecoat without revealing too much of her body.

'If you were a gentleman you'd turn away,' she snapped.

'It's far too diverting a spectacle,' he laughed, but turned from her all the same.

He went into the little room on hearing the heavy tread of the farmer on the path outside.

'Sorry to trouble you, Miss Hansford,' called Mr Chesworth, at the same time knocking loudly on her door. 'But the ewe has taken refuge under the caravan, and I didn't want to start messing about underneath without letting you know. She's been chased by the fox and is very frightened.'

'Thank you very much, Mr Chesworth.' How calm

and almost colourless her voice! Little did he know what he had interrupted!

'It's all right for me to try to get her out?'

'Of course.' She was out of bed and at the door. But then she remembered the key. Darius already had it in his hand when she tapped softly on his door.

'I'd keep it if I thought you'd not call out for his help,' he said, a question in his eyes which brought the colour flooding to her cheeks.

'I should poke my head through the window and say, "Mr Chesworth, there's a man in my caravan who's trying to molest me——"'

'All right,' he cut in with a low laugh. 'First round to you, my dear.' The key changed hands immediately.

'I'll have my clothes as well,' she said challengingly, a sparkle in her eye.

He shrugged, and gestured. Raine gathered up what he had placed on a chair and went out, closing the door behind her.

'Don't hurry, Mr Chesworth,' she was saying a moment later, in a carrying voice which Darius was meant to hear. 'You won't want to frighten the poor creature any more than she's frightened at present.'

'No, indeed. I might be quite a time persuading her to come out.' He was standing by the open door, looking rather troubled. Raine, well covered now and comfortable in her housecoat, looked down into his rugged face from the top step of the caravan.

'I'll get dressed and come and help you,' she offered, again in that carrying tone of voice.

'Well now, that's mighty obliging of you, Miss Hansford. Meanwhile, though, I'll be having a try to get her out.'

Within ten minutes Raine was washed and dressed,

with her hair brushed and her sandals rubbed over with a duster. She was almost ready to be off—and Darius Kallergis could get himself out of the situation as best he could!

It was another twenty minutes before the ewe was brought out from beneath the caravan, and because she wanted a little time to throw what clothes she had into the suitcase—most of her clothes being still in the bunk room—and gather together one or two other odds and ends, Raine suggested that Mr Chesworth should stay with the ewe and try to calm her.

'That's a good idea,' he agreed, patting the head of the animal.

Raine talked to him through the open door until she was ready to leave the caravan.

'I'm having to leave a little before I intended,' she smiled when eventually she appeared in the open, suitcase in hand.

'Oh, that's a pity. My wife did say as someone had brought you an urgent message last evening.'

'Yes, that's right.' So the Greek had done her a good turn, in one way, since Mr Chesworth was not now curious as to her change of plan.

'So you're going right away? You'll be catching the eight-fifteen, then?'

'Yes.' So there was a train at eight-fifteen. How very convenient.

'I'll get the lad to drive you to the station,' offered Mr Chesworth, glancing at his watch. 'It's early to get a taxi; they don't like coming all the way up here anyway. One fellow says as it's damaging to his springs. Has an ancient vehicle, though. You're ready right now?'

She nodded her head.

'Yes, quite ready.'

43

'Then come along down, and I'll find that lad of mine.'

Raine glanced at the door, and then at the key in her hand.

'I wonder if your wife would do me a favour?' she said.

'I'll be surprised if she won't, Miss Hansford,' he returned with a smile.

'Well, with having to leave in such a hurry, I've left food about. If she would remove it—and perhaps find a use for things like tea and sugar and the packets of biscuits—and lock the door, I'd be most grateful. And if you'd then post on the key to me?'

'Of course. Give the lad your address before he leaves you at the station.'

She thought about the girl who had lent her the caravan; she would naturally expect it to be left clean and tidy, and so Raine had already planned to come up next week-end and do what was necessary. Meanwhile, she could explain to the girl that she had had to come away in such a hurry that she could not clean the van and, therefore, she wished to retain the key until this was done.

She handed the key to Mr Chesworth, who put it carefully into his pocket.

'Off we go, then. I think the ewe will be all right now.' Mr Chesworth looked down at it. It was nibbling grass contentedly, and one or two more sheep had appeared. 'Can I take that suitcase for you?'

'Thank you very much.' She handed it to him, then said, 'Oh, just a moment. I've forgotten something,' and she went back into the caravan.

'You'd better get out as quickly as you can,' she advised when, after knocking softly on the door of the bunk room, she saw it open a little. 'I've given the key——'

'I heard!' Darius cut in, and she could not tell if he were angry or amused. 'Enjoy your freedom, my dear— but remember my warning! I shall have you for my own, make no mistake about that!'

A fortnight passed uneventfully and often when she tried to look back and bring those incredible scenes in- to focus, Raine found herself saying,

'If I weren't so confident of my sanity I'd begin to suspect myself of indulging in fantasy!'

Drena came one evening, asking about the broken engagement. But as she was delighted that her sister was not going to marry into so snobbish a family, Drena refrained from inquiring too deeply about it.

'We weren't really suited,' Raine had said. 'You were right, Drena, when you said he didn't love me.'

'Did you want him to love you? It always seemed to me that you didn't care one way or the other.'

Raine laughed. It was a strange thing, but quite often the good life she had lost did not trouble her over- much. It was not as if she had ever really tasted it, so she could scarcely miss it. At other times, though, she would fume and seethe and wish with all her heart that she could have had an opportunity of paying Darius Kallergis back for what he had done to her.

'As you know, Drena, I'm not particularly interested in love.'

'Then you should be!' admonished her sister. 'It's the most wonderful, and satisfying, thing in the world!'

Raine became serious for a space.

'I'm glad that you're in love, Drena,' she said sin- cerely. 'You always look so happy and contented, as does Paul as well.'

'We find life so exciting, and money seems not to matter in the least. We both work and between us we manage to have everything we want.'

'But then, Drena, your wants are not very great.'

'Nor are yours, Raine.'

Raine looked at her and smiled.

'I almost had the good life, a life of luxury,' she reflected, and a tiny sigh escaped her.

'What good would that have done you?' retorted her sister derisively. 'You'd have been driven mad by that superior lot!'

Superior ... Yes, they were superior, and yet they all paled into insignificance beside the noble personality of the Greek. But then his background was far in advance of anything the Redmaynes had known—his ancient background, that was, for the Greeks were the originators of Western civilisation, their culture being unsurpassed by anything else in the world.

'Where are you going for your holidays?' Drena was asking just before she departed. 'If you like you can come with us. We're going to Scarborough.'

Raine thanked her but declined the invitation. She was restless and she felt she ought to take a holiday entirely alone, so that she could regain that placid state of which her recent experiences had robbed her.

Another week passed, and her restlessness increased rather than abated; she kept finding herself looking into the handsome yet austere face of the Greek, bringing it into focus unwillingly and yet deriving a strange kind of pleasure from doing so. She concluded at last that it was natural that she should continually be thinking about him, since his was the kind of personality which left its mark in any circumstances, while in those particular circumstances through which she had lived the mark would be bound to stamp itself indelibly upon her mind. The tumultous sensations through which she had passed because of his conduct, the temptations which frightened even while they thrilled and yet tormented her. If Mr Chesworth had not come along that morning...

So many thoughts, and often uncontrolled. She blushed on occasions when visions passed before her eyes ... visions of Darius Kallergis whose mastery had caused her to be afraid even of herself.

She often wondered about his home, in the mountains of Greece, in that region of wild country in which stood a great temple to Apollo, God of Light. Here was the centre of an ancient cult inspired by the Delphic mysteries. It had always sounded weird to Raine, a place where shadows lurked, and in them the spirits of ancient gods, pagan gods both good and evil.

'I'd have liked to go to Delphi,' she murmured pensively to herself, 'but there's no chance of that now.' Yet it would be a strange coincidence if she and he did happen to meet, for Raine would be there for a short time only—if she went at all, that was.

So restless did she become that eventually she decided to decorate her living-room, in order to occupy her mind during the evenings and week-ends. With the paint and wallpaper purchased, she got down to it at last. Susie from the flat above came in, frankly admitting that she wanted to see what was going on. Raine patiently carried on with her work while Susie, astonished at the expertise shown by Raine, stood and watched.

'I think I'll have a go at mine,' decided Susie when Raine had almost finished. 'Would you help me?'

'Of course,' replied Raine. 'When do you want to start?'

'Next week-end, if it's all right with you?'

47

And so it transpired that on the following Saturday afternoon when a big grey car drew up at the front of the house, Raine was not in her own flat, but in Susie's.

'There's someone at your door.' Susie had been making a cup of tea in her little kitchen which looked out on to the front garden of the house. And as usual she had looked through the window. 'At least, there's a car there.'

'At my door?' frowned Raine, who was up the ladder, a distemper brush in her hand. 'I'm not expecting anyone.'

'I can't see the owner,' called Susie, who had returned to the kitchen to take another look, 'but the car's a beauty!'

Joining her at the window, Raine looked down ... and suddenly the fine hairs on her forearms began to stand up.

Could it be the Greek? But no; he had returned to his home over a month ago, having written her, Raine, off as one of his failures.

'I don't know who it can be,' she said, fully aware that Susie's curiosity would be well and truly aroused. Susie had always been there, at the kitchen window, whenever Stephen's car had driven on to the small forecourt on which the big grey car now stood. She knew the engagement was broken and had asked questions, but Raine had been very firm with her, saying she had no intention of talking about her engagement to anyone at all. 'I'd better go down and find out who it is.' Unconsciously she brushed away several locks of hair which had fallen on to her face—and she left behind smears of pale blue colour-wash that had got on to her hands. Susie noticed this and laughed.

'It's to be hoped it's not your best boy-friend,' she

said jokingly, 'because your hair—if you'll excuse me saying so—is definitely a mess!'

Raine glanced down at the overall she had on; it too was smeared with paint, but she merely shrugged her shoulders and, with a word of apology to Susie, she left the upper flat and went down to her own. It had only one entrance, the front door and, key in hand, Raine came from the side of the house—from where a door opened on to the staircase which led to Susie's flat—to the front. She had rounded the corner when she stopped dead, every nerve in her body rioting.

'*You!*' she cried, cursing herself for her stupidity. She could so easily have told Susie that she was not intending to go down, as whoever it was at her door would only be a representative for something or other, or a canvasser for the central heating firm who kept on sending illustrated leaflets through the letter-box. Yes, she could very well have escaped a meeting with this man, especially as her first thought on actually seeing the car was that it might have brought the Greek here.

'You don't appear to be overjoyed at seeing me,' observed Darius, his critical eyes roving her from head to foot. 'And after I've travelled all the way from Greece to visit you. I'd have been here much sooner but the pressure of business prevented it. I could not get away until last night.'

Raine was white to the lips, and her hand clenched on the key so tightly that she felt it cutting into her flesh. Was this man intending to haunt her all her life? Wild thoughts careering around in her brain included such things as moving house, asking for police protection and inventing a couple of hefty brothers who would not hesitate to knock him about if he continued to molest their sister. But, most of all, she found herself wanting to pay him out for all he had done, and

49

was still doing. To have come all the way from Greece ... It was clear that he had no intention of accepting defeat, but neither had she. Here, she was safe, and she had no intention of ever creating a situation where he would be the one in complete control, as was the case at the caravan.

He was speaking into her thoughts, asking in that suave half-lazy manner if she were intending to keep him on the step.

She looked directly at him, her chin lifted, her eyes sparkling with anger.

'Yes, I am intending to keep you on the step. I'd be the world's greatest fool to risk asking you into my home.' She paused briefly, and then, 'What do you want? I'm very busy and have no time to waste talking to you—nor have I the inclination to do so.'

The black eyes kindled and in spite of herself she shivered.

'You're very arrogant, Raine.'

Impatiently she moved.

'I've asked you what you want. Make no mistake, I'm not intending either to ask you in, or to stand here talking to you.'

'I'd like to speak to you in private, Raine.' His voice was low, his accent scarcely discernible. 'I promise that you'll be quite safe.'

Raine shook her head vigorously. She was furious to realise that there was certainly something about this man which could cause a weakness within her. She knew it would be folly to ask him in, and yet she was admitting into her mind the idea that his promise was sincere, and that if she did ask him in, she would be safe, as he had said.

'We're private here——' She swept a hand, indicating the garden, and the path. 'No one ever comes here.'

Darius's eyes lifted and, following his glance, Raine saw Susie's fair head being withdrawn from outside the window, which she had obviously opened after Raine had left her flat.

'Your neighbour's more than a little interested in us, my dear,' he said with a contemptuous smile. 'And when you become heated your voice carries, as you very well know.'

'I'm not intending to become heated.'

'Perhaps not, but you will become heated.'

'Mr Kallergis,' she said impatiently, 'will you please accept that you are not coming into my home?'

'Mr Kallergis?' he repeated slowly, his straight black brows lifting a fraction. 'It's time you were calling me Darius, my love.'

'I'm not your love!'

'Didn't I say you'd become heated?' Again his eyes wandered to the open window above his head. 'I've promised that, if you ask me in, you'll be perfectly safe.' He looked into her eyes, his own wide and unflinching. 'You might not think so, Raine, but you can trust me. If I give my word, I keep to it.' She was shaking her dark head as he spoke; it was an automatic gesture, but it betrayed the fear that was still within her. 'I won't molest you,' he added earnestly. 'I'm a man of honour——'

'Honour?' she echoed, a gasp in her voice.

'I admit you've an excuse for doubting me——'

'Excuses—in the plural! You've several times molested me, on one occasion causing me to lose wealth and a title——'

'The wealth I can supply but not, I'm afraid, the title. However, in my own country I am well respected, and in consequence you will be also.'

Her eyes flickered at these words.

'I? Just what are you offering me?' she asked.

'I do not intend to talk out here.'

Raine hesitated, one part of her totally rejecting the idea of allowing him into her home, while the other part of her found something intriguing in the very fact that he was here, having travelled all the way from Greece just to see her. Added to this was a deep sense of curiosity as to what he was offering her. At last she looked up into his face, noting the firm jawline, the classical lines which had caught her attention from that very first glimpse she had had of him, when he entered the banqueting hall of her fiancé's house.

'You've made a firm promise not to touch me,' she said, and somehow she found herself unable to look into his face as she spoke, even though she desired to do so in order to watch his reaction to what she had said.

'Yes, Raine, I've made you a firm promise.'

'Not to touch me,' she insisted, glancing up.

Darius smiled faintly; she noted the slight softening of his sensuous mouth, the glimmer of amusement that took the metal from his eyes.

'I won't touch you ... unless you want me to.'

Her colour flared.

'Why should I want you to?'

He did not answer this, but repeated what he had just said. He would not touch her unless she wanted him to do so.

'Very well ...' Even now she was undecided, the cautious part of her sending out red lights of warning. 'I—I shall have to go up and tell my neighbour that I shan't be back to help for a while.'

Darius's eyes softened a little more.

'Do that by all means, my dear. Tell her to come down in ten minutes or so if you must, but I assure you there is no need for you to seek protection in this way.'

Raine's already heightened colour increased.

'You're very perceptive,' she said.

'You're an open book, Raine. And fear is written all over your face.'

'Does that surprise you?'

'No, dear, it doesn't,' he admitted, but without a trace of remorse or self-blame. 'However, I am not intending to hurt you, so your fear is quite unnecessary.'

Five minutes later she was seated opposite to him in her bright, newly-decorated sitting-room. He had glanced around on entering, had remarked on the one or two fine antiques which she possessed, and now he was talking to her, telling her even yet again that he and she were meant for one another, and that she need not fight against her fate, as it was futile for her to do so. Raine listened, then asked bluntly,

'I am to take it that you want me for your pillow friend? That's it, isn't it?' She watched his expression change rapidly to one of angry indignation and her wide brow creased in puzzlement. She could not have described the sensations which were passing through her, but the one which was strongest was the burning desire to pay him out for his part in the wreckage of her bright future.

'Where, might I ask,' he was saying with a kindling glance, 'did you hear that expression?'

'What expression?'

'Don't try my patience,' he said sternly. 'Pillow friend! Where did you hear it?'

'I can't remember. Does it matter?'

He looked at her, his mouth tight. She knew a strong desire to laugh, because it seemed so ludicrous for a man with his morals to be objecting to the use of the phrase.

'It does matter. I intensely dislike those words coming from lips as beautiful as yours.'

The compliment brought a tinge of colour to her cheeks.

Darius seemed fascinated by what he saw, although a dark frown touched his brow when his eyes rested on her hair. He began speaking again, and to her amazement he told her that it was a very different kind of relationship he wished to have with her. It was marriage he desired.

'Marriage ...?' The word seemed to magnify itself in her brain. He was willing to marry her. He had said he could supply the wealth that she had lost.

Raine drew a long breath, vitally aware that her one dominating thought was still that of paying him out for what he had done to her. The scene in the caravan came vividly into the forefront of her mind; she lived again that interlude when, clad only in a sheet, she had been completely at his mercy, and saved only by the timely appearance of the farmer.

'Yes, my love, marriage.' Darius's soft voice broke into her reflections and she glanced at him across the room. 'I'll teach you to love me, Raine,' he added, then lapsed into silence.

Love! Did he really believe that she could ever love him after what he had done? Love a pagan like him—with his primitive instincts? She could have laughed in his face, but she refrained. The idea had come to her suddenly, an idea conceived by her desire for revenge, and strengthened by the knowledge that Darius was a wealthy man.

'Tell me about yourself,' she invited. 'I know nothing, except that you come from Delphi, of course.'

'There isn't much to tell, my love. I'm in the wine business, and I own a few ships——'

'A few?'

'Well, a fleet of pleasure cruisers, and a few larger vessels.'

'And ... your home?' She was not interested in his home, as she had no intention of ever living there.

'I think you'll like it,' he said, and now an edge of enthusiasm brought out the accent, most attractively, she had to own. 'It's a low white villa with a view to the mountains—the Phaedriades, from which, as you probably know, gushes forth the Castalian Spring——' He broke off. 'You probably *don't* know,' he said with a smile.

'I've heard a little about Delphi,' she said, her mind again reverting to the idea that had come to her.

Marry him, and leave him! But make him provide for her first.

She said, pretending to be thoughtful,

'Marriage is a very serious step——'

'You were on the point of taking that step when we first met,' he reminded her.

'Yes ...' Again she feigned a depth of thought. 'Stephen would have—er ...' She was, strangely, reluctant to lie, but she had no need to do so, as her hesitation told him all she had wanted to convey.

'He would have settled a sum of money on you?'

Again she was reluctant to lie—but she gave him a glance that was quite sufficient for him to draw the conclusion she desired him to draw.

'I shall do the same,' he promised. 'I shall settle it on you the moment we are married—— Well, a few moments later,' he amended. 'We'll have a lawyer handy and waiting.' He looked at her, rather anxiously, she thought, and wondered what his reaction would be were she to draw back at this stage and say she could not marry him. However, she had no intention of saying anything of the kind. Here was the opportunity of paying him back—an opportunity which she could scarcely believe had come her way.

But it had, and the confident, self-opinionated Darius Kallergis would be wishing he had never set eyes on her, much less treated her so brutally. 'Well, Raine,' he said presently, 'are you going to say yes?'

She gave a small sigh.

'I don't love you, Darius——' She stopped, then smiled. His name had come out so naturally, and she actually liked the sound of it as it left her lips.

'I don't expect you to love me, after what I've done,' he said frankly. 'But love will come. I shall not be long in making you love me.'

She glanced down, lowering her long dark lashes. What a conceited creature he was! She had no compunction at all at what she was planning. It was high time his pride was brought down into the dust. She could not help a feeling of exultation when she thought of his being tied to her, yet being on his own. She doubted very much that he would want a divorce. The Greeks were known to be against the casual breaking of a marriage. No, he would remain tied to her for the whole of his life—which meant he would never have a son, and to have a son and heir was of the most profound importance to every Greek male.

'If you are satisfied with that sort of a bargain——?' she began, assuming a sort of shy hesitancy. 'Then—Darius, I will marry you.'

At this he rose, although a deep silence remained long after she had spoken. He came towards her and she rose from her chair.

'Can we seal that with a kiss?' he asked, and she found it very strange indeed for him to be asking, instead of demanding.

She nodded her head, aware that she was experiencing the mixed feelings of wanting to repel him even while she tilted her face, almost inviting his kiss.

'This is what you meant when you said you'd not touch me unless I wanted you to?'

His smile was her answer as, taking her in his arms, he bent his head and pressed his lips to hers.

When presently he drew away she stared up at him, aware, for the first time, that this pagan from the East could be gentle!

CHAPTER FOUR

THEY were married four days later, with only Drena and her husband present. So very different from the fashionable wedding to which, so short a time ago, Raine had been eagerly looking forward.

'I'm not altogether happy,' Drena had said after first learning that Raine was to be married to a Greek. 'However, he's better than that awful Stephen. I don't suppose you're in love with this foreigner, though?'

'Not in the least,' was Raine's careless rejoinder. 'Nor have I any intention of ever trying to love him.'

'Oh, well,' sighed Drena, 'I suppose you know what you're doing.'

As promised, Darius had a lawyer handy, and the sum made over to her caused Raine's eyes to open very wide indeed. Darius had previously mentioned a sum of money, with which she had been more than satisfied, but he later said he intended to increase the original amount.

They were to spend the first night of their honeymoon at a London hotel, but it had not been Raine's intention to get even as far as entering the hotel. She had meant to give Darius the slip long before then. However, she found that it was not so easy, since he had ordered a meal for the four of them, at a local hotel, and after that he drove them all back to Raine's flat, where her sister helped her to change her clothes and then finished her packing for her.

'Write often, won't you?' said Drena. 'And invite us over to visit you.'

Raine felt a fraud and for a moment was tempted to let Drena into the secret. But she decided that the time was not yet. Tomorrow Drena and her husband would know all there was to know. For the present she merely replied,

'I'll be in touch very soon, Drena.'

Darius, talking to Paul in the sitting-room, turned his head immediately his wife entered, and the admiration that lit his eyes was there for all to see.

'Ready, my love?'

Raine, pale and feeling slightly off-colour, nodded and smiled, then cast a glance in her sister's direction.

'Yes, Darius, I'm ready.'

He drove all the way to London, chatting for a while, then lapsing into silence. Now and then he would mention something about his home, but he did say he would like it all to be a surprise for her. He seemed so happy, like a boy, almost, instead of a man in his thirties. So different from the savage who had forced his kisses on her and arrogantly declared that she would be his. He was a strange mixture, she decided, comparing him now to what he had been on those accasions when he had terrified her, portraying as he had such fierce, primitive traits, forcing her to bend to his will. That he had a wild, unquenchable desire for her was more than evident by the fact of his going to the unexpected lengths of marriage. Marriage ... Raine gave an involuntary shudder as she tried, for one fleeting moment, to visualise her life as his wife. Subjugated, his slave. Well, she never would be his wife—except in name, of course —and as she pictured his fury on discovering he'd been duped, she prayed that, once she had got away, he would never catch up with her again.

When eventually they did go to their suite, Raine was

becoming desperate. She had previously planned on either making her escape some time between the actual ceremony and the time for their departure for London. The meal ordered by Darius for them precluded any chance of this. Then he had driven them to London in the hired car instead of using the train as she had expected he would. If he had done this then she could have got up just before a stop, saying she was wanting to wash her hands or comb her hair—and she would have got off the train.

'What is it, my dear?' He came to her in the bedroom and took her hands in his. 'You look pale, and—well, a little troubled?'

With an effort she produced a smile.

'Just a little tired, Darius, that's all.'

'Too much to do in one day? I should not have taken you dancing, should I?'

'I enjoyed it,' she said, and it could have been the truth, had her mind not been disturbed by the possibility of her not being able to make her escape.

He kissed her gently, then told her to go through to the bathroom first, and then she could get into bed. He'd be a little time, he said, because he intended having a shave.

She came from the bathroom in a lovely negligée, her hair shining from the brushing she had given it.

'I'll not be as long as I thought,' he declared, but his eyes were laughing and she knew he was only teasing her.

She got into bed, her heart throbbing madly at the idea of what she was about to do. It was all so vague, now that she had no firm plan in her mind. However, no sooner had Darius disappeared into the bathroom than she was up. Slipping off her nightgown, she donned her clothes faster than at any other time in her life, even faster than on that occasion at the caravan. Silenty she reached for her coat after having deposited the note she had already written—telling her husband that she had married him for revenge only, and bragging over her cleverness in getting him to sign the money over to her—on the dressing-table by the mirror, and then, grabbing her handbag and suitcase, she went softly from the bedroom to the lounge and then out into the corridor. It was thickly carpeted and she raced along it towards the lift, which took an eternity in coming. Her nerves were rioting as she waited, expecting every moment to see her husband come from their suite and drag her back to the bedroom. At the very idea of his fury she went white. The lift came at last, but she still did not feel safe. She had a vague notion of the night porter deciding to call Darius and tell him his wife was here, in the lobby, asking for a taxi.

But all went well; the taxi was there and she got straight into it, telling the driver to drop her at another hotel. From there she took another taxi, then another, aware that all these precautions were quite unnecessary, but fear of capture drove her to extremes. She ended up at a small hotel in Earls Court and finally she slept.

'You mean you've left him already?' It was the following day and Raine, unwilling to venture home or even to call on her sister, had telephoned Drena from a small, rather shabby establishment carrying the weather-worn sign,

'Frisby's Boarding House. Bed and Breakfast. Rooms.'

'Yes, I intended leaving him. Drena, I must talk to you.'

'You want me to come to this place, I presume?'

'I'm glad you catch on quickly,' returned Raine with a laugh which quite naturally astonished her sister.

'What's the address again?'

Raine gave it to her.

'Not a word to Paul, remember.'

'I wouldn't dare tell him. He'd forbid me to see you, declaring you to be mad!'

'Thanks! I'm very sane, and very delighted with what I've done. However, that's all I'm saying at present. When will you be here?'

'In about an hour. Paul's got the car in pieces—well, it seems it's in pieces! So I'll have to come on the bus.'

It was Saturday afternoon and the buses were not so plentiful as in the week, but Drena managed to get to the boarding house within an hour and a half.

'Lord,' she exclaimed on seeing her sister's room, 'this isn't what you're used to!'

Raine only laughed.

'I'm not troubled. I took this place because it's not too far from you. I thought I owed it to you to tell you everything.' And without any hesitation she related the whole story from beginning to end. Drena's face underwent many changes of expression and when at last Raine stopped speaking she just sat there, dumbfounded by it all.

'It's like something out of a play,' she managed at length. 'Fiction rather than fact.'

Raine nodded her head.

'Do you blame me for getting my own back?' she asked, watching her sister closely.

'No, I don't think I do—although I myself would never have had the courage to have done it.'

'I didn't really have courage,' admitted Raine. 'I was terrified last night.'

'I can imagine!' Drena looked at her, sipping the

tea which the landlady had provided. 'What are your plans now? You're rich, I suppose?'

'Not rich, but fairly well off. I'm going to invest most of what Darius has given me——'

'You're sure you'll have that money? I mean—he could stop the cheque, couldn't he?'

'It was a cash transfer; the money went straight into my bank. Darius said I could transfer it to Greece later.'

'So he had money in this country, obviously?'

Raine nodded.

'Yes, he must have done.'

'You're intending to invest it, you were saying?'

'That's right.'

'And you're moving from your flat?'

'I shall have to.' Involuntarily Raine shuddered and a heavy frown came to her sister's forehead.

'He sounds a beast,' she said, anger creeping into her voice.

'Strangely,' mused Raine, 'he can be gentle as well.'

Drena looked curiously at her.

'You don't ... like him, just a little?'

'Is it feasible that I could?' returned Raine with a lift of her brows.

'He must never find you.'

'If he ever does he'll probably murder me,' she said, and it was Drena's turn to shudder.

'You shouldn't have got yourself mixed up with him, Raine.'

'How could I have done otherwise?'

'No, I can see how it was. What with him following you to the caravan, and then taking all the trouble to come over here. He's done a good deal of chasing, you must admit.'

'I do.'

'To be candid, Raine, I feel he's in love with you.'

'In love!' scoffed Raine with a lift of her brows. 'It's desire—nothing more nor less.'

'Did he ask you to have an affair?' Drena wanted to know, a curious tone in her voice.

'No, he didn't.'

'That's strange, isn't it?'

'I feel he knew for sure that he'd not get me without marriage.'

'Would he go to the lengths of marriage just for desire?'

'I don't know.' The subject was becoming embarrassing and Raine changed it. 'As to where I shall go, Drena, I haven't decided. But I thought I'd buy myself a little cottage somewhere in the country.'

Her sister gave a deep sigh, shaking her head and frowning.

'You can't shut yourself off like that, Raine. You enjoyed being engaged to Stephen, and having what you called the good life.'

'I like the country, you know I do.'

'But you're young!'

'What of it? I shall have my cottage in the country and breed dogs, or something like that.'

'You'll get fed up in no time at all, and want to go back to work.'

'If I do want to get a job there'll be nothing to stop me. I can afford a car now, so I shall be able to commute.'

Drena looked at her, watching the movement of her long slender hands as she poured out their second cup of tea.

'You seem to have it all worked out, Raine, but I just can't see it going the way you expect, Don't you ever want to get married?'

At this Raine gave a gust of laughter.

'I am married, you idiot! You attended my wedding yesterday!'

'Only yesterday. And you're here, in this poky little room, all on your own.'

For a moment Raine could find nothing to say. Not for one moment would she have admitted it, but she was feeling the first tinge of apprehension at what she had done. Her life had been smooth before she met Stephen, and it would have continued to be smooth after the engagement was broken—if she had steered clear of Darius Kallergis—or rather, if Darius Kallergis had left her alone! Yes, everything was his fault, she tried to convince herself ... but deep within her this doubt had been born. She knew she could have acted very differently. No man, and especially a foreigner, was allowed to persecute anyone. She could have sent him away, and made sure he did not molest her ever again. Would he look for her? Probably, but he would never find her; Raine decided she would make quite sure of that.

Eventually it was time for Drena to leave, She was troubled, but not unduly so, as Raine had assured her that she would be managing very well.

'We'll keep in touch by phone,' said Drena as she and Raine walked to the bus stop. 'I daren't tell Paul about this—not yet.'

'I understand. Being a man, he wouldn't approve of what I've done.'

'It's true; he wouldn't.'

Raine saw her on to the bus, waved as it drew away, then turned and strolled slowly back to her room.

It was a month later and Raine had been incredibly fortunate in finding the cottage she had wanted. She had bought a car, and some furniture; she had the garden landscaped by an expert, and had an orchard planted. This took time, but as the cottage was untenanted she was able to take possession as soon as she had paid for it.

Drena took a day off work to visit her, and was thrilled with it all.

'Oh, but if we could only have found a place like this!' she cried as, wandering around the outside on this lovely sunny day in August, she stopped now and then to smell the old-fashioned roses that—judging by the size of the trees—had been in the garden for a great number of years. 'You're lucky, Raine!'

'I know. I'm very well satisfied with myself, Drena.'

'But you've become so hard.' Drena looked apologetically at her. 'It isn't like you to think of the material things of life.'

'I've been thinking of the material things of life for some time,' Raine was quick to remind her. 'I got engaged to Stephen merely to gain the material things of life.' Yes, she told herself, the material things of life were all that mattered!

But the moment her sister had left she sat down, on a little seat in the garden, and somehow there was a great deal that was missing. It was not that she felt lonely; far from it. She had always liked her own company. The life she had been forced to lead as a child, and later, when she was in her teens, had been one of isolation at times. She and Drena had been the best of friends, but inevitably each had made their separate friends as the years went by, and there were numerous occasions when Drena would be on her own, while Raine was with a friend. Then it would be Raine's turn to find herself alone. Had their parents made for them the kind of happy family life enjoyed by their friends and schoolmates, then perhaps their personalities would have de-

66

veloped along slightly different lines from what they had done. As it was, both Drena and Raine found no hardship in being alone.

And so, as she sat there on the little seat, with the scents from her old-fashioned English garden assailing her nostrils, Raine began an attempt to analyse her new life, and to find out just what was missing.

Perhaps, she decided in the end, she ought to get another job.

This she did, travelling into town each day and returning in the late afternoon. Inevitably her husband would intrude into her thoughts and she would in imagination see his fury on discovering that she had slipped away—on his wedding night! What a shock, and a disappointment.

However, he had neither contacted Drena nor been to Raine's flat, so it was logical to assume that he had accepted defeat, deciding that he might search for months and never find his wife. But even if he did there was no law on earth that could make her live with him. Raine supposed he had gnashed his teeth time and time again over the money he had been fool enough to give her.

She had been working for just over a fortnight when, after going on to see a film after leaving the office, she arrived home when dusk was falling. On entering her little cottage she stopped abruptly in the hallway, her nerves tingling. She felt a strange compulsion to turn around and run.

'Don't be absurd,' she said to herself, but even then she did not move, and she found her mind leaping ahead to the possibility of there being a burglar in the house. Yet she had heard no sound, and nothing unusual had caught her eye.

She moved at last, into the low, oak-beamed parlour

—then stopped again, every vestige of colour leaving her face.

'So we meet again—wife!' The last word was a snarl, guttural as that of an animal about to rob its prey of life.

'I—you—h-how d-did——?' She got no further; with the swiftness of a jungle cat he was beside her, taking her shoulders in a cruel and bruising grip.

'Did you think for one moment that I wouldn't find you!' He shook her unmercifully, then flung her on to the couch. Standing menacingly over her, he said, his face terrible to see, his lips drawn back to reveal his strong white teeth, 'The reckoning was bound to come, Raine. Had you taken the trouble to know me better you'd never have taken the risk that you did. I said you were mine, that I should have you in the end—and I *shall*!'

An unbelievable weakness was spreading over her; she made no attempt to rise, aware that she had no power to move, even if he had not been standing above her.

'Darius,' she managed at last, 'I'll g-give you all—all the money b-back——'

His harsh and ruthless laugh cut into her faltering words and at the same time his hand shot out and she was jerked to her feet.

'Money! You think of nothing else! It isn't money I want, wife, it's you!'

She swayed dizzily, wondering if this was the end, if he would use these long slender fingers which were at present digging into her shoulders, to strangle the very life out of her. Terror she had known before, in the caravan, but now it brought with it a physical sickness born of utter hopelessness and resignation. He would injure her in some way, she felt absolutely sure of it.

However, self-preservation was strong within her and she tried to plead with him. It was to no avail. His brutal kisses were only a prelude to the unbridled savagery of the lovemaking that came later, when, lifting her as if she were no heavier than a kitten, he carried her up to the dainty bedroom she had so recently furnished for herself.

She awoke to the painful discovery that her head was throbbing with a dull yet heavy ache. Dawn had brought its pearl-grey light to the sky, but the room was still dark. Memory flooded in and she rose, without a glance at the black head resting so peacefully on the pillow.

Wrapped in her housecoat, she went from the room, silently descending the stairs, her clothes under her arm. She turned at the foot to glance back, then hurriedly dressed. Her little car was in the drive, where she had left it and she went out to it. A voice from above said quietly,

'It's out of action, my dear. You'll leave here only with your husband.'

She looked up at the window, vaguely noticing the pretty lace curtains with their big pink bows holding them in place. The curtains were for effect only, as the cottage was entirely on its own, approached from the road by a long tree-lined drive.

She accepted her husband's word regarding the car, although it did strike her that, if he had put it out of order, then he must have got up in the middle of the night to do it. However, as she was under no illusions about the impossibility of escape now that he was awake, she went back into the cottage and sat down. Darius appeared, clad in the black and red dressing-gown, a sneer of triumph on his face.

The expression riled her, and she lifted her chin and said,

'What did you mean—I'd leave here only with you?'

'Exactly what I said.' He was standing a few feet from her, his black eyes fixing hers—as a stoat fixes a poor little rabbit, she thought, trying to draw her eyes away, but without success.

'You can't force me to go to Greece with you.'

'Can't I?' He seemed to draw an impatient breath. 'How little you know me, Raine. If you would heed my words of advice and warning you'd practise greater caution.'

'I'm English,' she reminded him. 'You'd find it impossible to get me out of the country against my will.'

He ignored that and said,

'I expect you have plenty of food in the house?'

'Yes, of course I have.' She looked at him with an expression that was half puzzled, half suspicious. 'Are you contemplating staying here for some time?'

'Only for a brief honeymoon—to make up for the one we missed. If you have eggs, you can boil me a couple. I'll have toast and marmalade as well, and strong black coffee.'

Raine stayed where she was.

'I'm not your servant,' she told him defiantly.

'You're my wife.' So soft the tone, but dangerously so. 'And you will learn, right now, that obedience to my wishes is vital for your comfort.'

She swallowed hard.

'Aren't you capable of boiling yourself two eggs?' she asked.

Her husband's black eyes should have been warning enough, but the compression of his mouth was supplementary to his determination to show her who was master.

'Raine ... do as I bid you.'

She was white to the lips, and she knew she must give way in the end, but she could not bring herself to do so without a fight.

'I'm not taking orders from you, Darius. In Greece you might treat your women like servants, but——' He stopped her by jerking her roughly to her feet.

'In there—and have my breakfast on the table by the time I'm dressed!' He propelled her to the kitchen door, then gave her a little shove. 'I shall be no more than ten minutes!' He paused a moment. 'And have some yourself——'

'I don't want anything to eat! Even you can't force food down my throat!'

'Can't I?' he returned with grim amusement. 'Try me, Raine, and you'll see whether I can or not!'

Two days passed, with Raine asking Darius about his intentions and he always answering curtly,

'That's my business. You've forfeited the right to share confidences with me.'

'We can't stay here, in this cottage, indefinitely.'

'I haven't any intention of doing so,' was all he would say in response to this statement. He spent some considerable time on her telephone, with the hall door closed, so that there was no possibility of her overhearing the conversations he was having. She had asked how he had found her and was told that he had employed a private detective to trace her. He had been forced to return to Greece to attend to some business matters and the detective had had orders to contact him when, and if, he should discover her whereabouts.

'So you see,' he added with a sneer, 'you underrate my ability to substantiate any statements I might make.

71

I said you'd never escape me, and you won't ... not as long as you live.'

Her heart sank at these words, for she felt certain now that he was more than capable of finding her, no matter where she should try to hide herself.

But the thought of spending the rest of her life with him appalled her; he was a savage, ruthless and domineering. This small sample had been more than enough to convince her that she would rather die than go on like this to the end of her life.

On the morning of the third day he informed her that they would be leaving that night for his home in Greece.

'You can't make me go with you,' she told him, but, strangely, without the conviction which she would have liked to insert into her voice.

'You'll learn one day,' was his impatient rejoinder, 'that plans which I make never go awry.'

She did not argue, but considered him pompous and conceited to make a declaration like that. Some day his plans would go awry—everybody's did at one time or another.

Obviously she was interested in this present plan of his, the plan to get her out of the country. She had a passport in her maiden name and she had no intention of handing it over to him. He had made her pack two suitcases, and had stood over her while she wrote a letter to her sister, giving her authority to sell the cottage or, alternatively, she and Paul could live in it. This latter had been inserted because Raine had happened to mention her sister's enthusiasm for the cottage, and her wish that she and her husband could have found such a place.

In all, everything had been done, but Raine was still optimistic about effecting an escape, as she could not by any stretch of imagination see herself being abducted —which was what it would amount to if she was taken away against her will.

At ten o'clock a large car drove right up to the front of the cottage.

'The driver is Angelos, a servant of mine,' Darius informed her even before the man had alighted from the car. 'He's the skipper of the boat which will take us to Greece.' So calm, so efficient. Raine's heart sank and all hope fled. His Greek servant driving the car; this man Angelos would be there if she made any move to escape as she was taken from the car to the boat. She recalled Darius's telling her that he owned, among other things, a fleet of pleasure cruisers. He had later explained that people usually formed parties and then chartered a boat and crew to take them round the Mediterranean, calling at the Greek islands. He had said that the harbour of Mandraki, in Rhodes, was a favourite place for his pleasure boats to be moored.

Raine concluded that it would be such a boat on which her husband proposed to take her out of the country.

'This, then,' she said at length, 'is the reason for all the telephone calls you've been making?'

'Yes. Angelos has flown over from Greece. He arranged for one of my boats to be at Southampton to take us home. The crew are on board, but the captain had earlier been taken ill and flown to his home on the island of Crete.' Darius's voice was icily polite, his gaze hard and cold. 'If you cause any trouble, Raine, you'll upset no one but yourself. You're my wife; you married me willingly. Therefore your place is with me, in my country, and that is where you will spend the rest of your life. Angelos knows that you might resist being taken on to the boat——'

'You told him!' she said sharply. The very idea of a Greek servant knowing that she was being forcibly taken to his home by her husband filled her with angry humiliation.

'It was necessary—unfortunately. You've asked for everything,' he told her harshly, noting her expression. 'If you suffer embarrassment then just try to remember that you've brought it all on yourself.'

She flared, bitter hatred of him bringing a hard, unmusical pitch to her voice.

'If you had left me alone at the beginning none of this would have happened! Why blame me for it all?'

His dark eyes raked her contemptuously.

'Keep your voice down! My wife does not conduct herself like a noisy peasant woman! Raise your voice like that again and you'll smart for it! Yes, blush! I enjoy witnessing your discomfiture. As for my blaming you for it all,' he went on, reverting to what she had said, 'I married you in good faith, offering you what I had offered no other woman in my life. You cheated, and you'll pay for that—pay so dearly that you will wish with all your heart you'd never been born!'

Raine went white. What had this fiend in store for her, once he got her to his home in the wild mountains of Delphi? Tears stung her eyes, but she would not allow them to fall. He should not enjoy witnessing her fear and unhappiness.

The servant was waiting respectfully by the car when Darius opened the cottage door.

'These bags,' said Darius curtly, gesturing with his hand. There were two of his and two of hers. 'You have the letter?' he asked Raine, then ordered her to hand it to the servant. It was to her sister; the man took it and put it in his pocket. The order for him to stop and

74

post it had obviously already been given over the telephone.

Darius Kallergis thought of everything.

With the suitcases in the boot of the car, he locked the door of the cottage and put the key under a rockery stone. Raine had included this hiding place in her letter to Drena.

'Get in,' ordered Darius and, with her hopes all vanquished, she obeyed, glancing at the man standing almost to attention by the car door. His eyes never wavered, yet she sensed his deep interest in his master's wife, a wife who quite plainly did not go with her husband willingly.

Darius got in beside her, while Angelos, after closing the door, got into the driver's seat.

'What are you thinking about?' The question came from Darius after a long silence, when the car was speeding along the motorway, its headlights flaring out in front of it.

Raine told him the truth, that she was wondering how it was that for three whole days he had not only kept her prisoner in her own house, but had managed to keep her from speaking either to the postman, who had called twice, or on the telephone.

'It is natural that I should keep a close surveillance on you,' he said coldly, 'after what you had done to me before.'

She glanced swiftly at him, frowning at the idea that a hint of a tremor had entered his voice. He would have been furious about her running away, but certainly not hurt!

It seemed an eternity that they had been in the car, travelling through the darkness, but at last she saw the sea, shimmering in the moonlight.

'We're—we're h-here,' she whispered huskily. 'Darius, I——'

'One word from you as we get on to the boat, and you'll be picked up like a sack and carried aboard. Understand?' His hand was already gripping her wrist as the car began to slow down, right by a jetty. 'I said, do you understand!'

She nodded, scarcely able to articulate words, so lost and hopeless did she feel.

'Yes—yes, Darius, I understand.'

CHAPTER FIVE

THE voyage was over; the boat was moored at a little jetty just south of the port of Itea where a car was waiting, having been brought there by another Greek servant whom Darius introduced as Giorgios. Raine got into the car, followed closely by her husband. The driver was soon drawing away, on to a road fringed by olive trees. Despite her situation Raine could not remain insensible to the beauty of the countryside, especially when they drove further inland, alongside a vast unbroken sea of olives. This, Darius curtly informed her, was the sacred Plain of Amphissa.

'How far have we to drive to get to your home?' she asked.

'Fourteen miles.'

'The scenery's beautiful,' she commented after a long while.

Darius made no answer.

'What's the name of this village we're now passing through?' she inquired of him on another occasion.

'Khrison,' was his brief reply.

'What are those men doing?'

Her husband frowned as if his patience were running out.

'What men?'

'Those over there—sitting at that table under a tree.'

'Playing *tavla*.'

'It's a game?'

He ignored that and for the rest of the journey there was silence between them.

'This is our home.' Darius broke the silence only when the car, having swept along a winding drive fringed with exotic trees and bushes, had slid to a standstill before the imposing entrance to the villa.

'It's very lovely.' Raine could not hold back her appreciation, for the white house with its bright blue shutters and marble steps leading up to the front door was a most delightful picture, especially as it was set amid magnificent gardens which had obviously received regular care and attention.

Darius said nothing and she turned her head to glance at him. A tiny gasp was swiftly suppressed. His face was grim and drawn—as if he were suffering some sort of pain, but whether it was physical or mental pain she could not have said.

He took her into the house, through a high arched hallway towards the room at the far end, a large room which had two dressing-rooms off it, and a delightful coral and white bathroom with gold-plated fittings. The view was over the gardens and the sweep of a smooth green lawn to the orchard beyond where grew oranges and lemons and the delicious seedless clementines.

Raine turned from the scene outside, and glanced around the room. The carpet was white, the furniture of bird's-eye walnut. The bed, very wide and long, had a quilted velvet headboard in a delicate shade of lilac; the chairs and stool matched this headboard, while the long velvet drapes were of white to match the carpet.

She looked up at her husband, bewilderment in her eyes.

'It all looks so new,' she pointed out. 'Has it not been used before?'

'I did it for us.'

'You——!' She stared at him in disbelief. 'But how

could you have done it for us? I mean—when did you do it?'

'I did it when I decided to marry you.'

She gasped. So calmly he spoke of when *he* had decided to marry her. No thought that she might wish to be consulted. Anger rose but was suppressed. During those three days when he had her prisoner at the cottage she had witnessed his temper; she had no desire for a repetition.

'So you did this after you came home the first time, and before you returned to England?'

He nodded.

'After the caravan episode. I decided that it would have to be marriage, and so I had this all done by a firm in Athens. I trust it meets with your approval?' he added with a sudden sneer.

She swallowed and turned away. Such a beautiful home. She preferred it to the stately pile that was Redmayne House. It was more warm and welcoming, less grand and overpowering. It was light and airy, with flowers everywhere. Climbing up the two pillars on the balcony were lovely bougainvillaea vines, one crimson and the other a brilliant orange. It struck her that these would be seen from the bed, if the curtains were open, that was.

Darius was speaking, his deep, accented voice stern to the point of harshness.

'If you are plotting to escape me, Raine, then I advise you to think again. I believe you know by now that what I say I mean. You're mine—and mine you shall remain!'

Her face lost a little of its colour. She thought of his savagery, his total disregard for her feelings, his arrogant domination of her both physically and mentally.

'I can't stay with you for ever,' she had to say, because she was unable to hold it back. 'Life would be—hell.'

'Thanks! You deserve all you've got. You're a cheat, Raine, and I have my own way of dealing with cheats!' His black eyes bored into her, examining her very soul. 'You've deliberately robbed me, but now I shall take what I've paid for. You spoke of pillow friends. You can consider yourself as just that—a pillow friend!' Although his words were harsh, there was a faintly bitter curve to his mouth, and a brooding pause ensued before he added, 'As my pillow friend you will not, of course, enjoy the advantages which you would have enjoyed as my wife.'

A little more colour left her face. She felt trapped at this moment, but at the back of her mind there lingered the certainty of escape. It was impossible for him to keep her here indefinitely.

'Shall we go?' Darius was saying, and she nodded. 'I'll show you the rest of the house.'

It was all as beautiful as the bedroom, tastefully furnished and decorated, with long drapes to every window and expensive carpets on the floors. Patios and verandahs were embellished with brilliantly-coloured subtropical flowers or vines, and in the rooms themselves flowers invariably held an important place. She saw two gardeners outside, in the extensive shrubbery which ran the full length of the back garden. In the house, Darius told her, were the wives of these two men, Katina and Nicoleta, who did the cleaning and cooking.

Raine turned to him when presently they were on the patio.

'What is there for me to do, then?' The very idea of idleness daunted her; she must have something to occupy her mind, if only to help her forget for a while the terrible mess she had made of her life.

Her husband looked down at her with a prolonged unsmiling stare which was so disconcerting that she had a sudden desire to turn and run from him.

'Your role will be to look beautiful ... and tempting. You'll satisfy my more basic needs——'

'Do you have to speak like this!' she broke in fiercely. 'You've just said I'll be your pillow friend! Do you need to enlarge on that?' Anger brought back the colour to her cheeks and his eyes kindled.

'Red-faced women are always unattractive,' he told her icily. 'Learn to control your temper—or I shall be compelled to control it for you!'

She flashed him a venomous glance.

'You seem to forget that I'm English! I happen to possess a little spirit!—not like your subjugated Greek women who are classed as inferior to the male.'

'So you've been reading, have you?'

'Most people know that women from the East are classed as inferior.'

'They are given their place, and they accept that their menfolk are the masters.' He was showing a trace of amusement now, and triumph too. It was plain that he derived some measure of satisfaction from his treatment of her. Revenge was his aim and as yet the treatment was mild ... but what would he be like later? His threats had been serious threats; Raine was under no illusions about this. She recalled vividly his treatment of her during those three days which he always referred to as their belated honeymoon. His prisoner, she had no escape or defence from his primitive lovemaking; he had conquered her in revenge, subjugated her in hate.

And now he had her here in Greece, land of pagan gods and sleeping spirits, land where the man was the master, his word the law which his womenfolk obeyed.

In an attempt to throw off her depressing thoughts,

she brought back the subject to that of her employment.

'I must be occupied,' she went on. 'There must be some work I can do?'

Darius's black eyes fixed hers.

'You'll do as I say—look beautiful.' He stopped a moment. 'Although I've said you'll be my pillow friend,' he continued, 'I shall of course refer to you as my wife——'

'I should hope you would!' she interrupted hotly.

'Be very careful,' her husband warned in a dangerously quiet voice. 'Women here don't interrupt when their husbands are speaking.' His eyes had narrowed, his mouth gone tight. 'As I was saying, I shall refer to you as my wife, and myself as your husband.' He paused and she waited for him to continue with what he himself had interrupted. 'You'll look beautiful for your husband—that is all you will be required to do. Working makes women ugly; their hands become enlarged, their faces drawn and their figures muscular.'

'So I'm to be a doll, am I?'

'Something like that,' he returned with a hint of amusement. 'Perhaps a "soft toy" would be a more descriptive way of putting it.'

A toy ... Plaything of this pagan Greek. Raine went hot all over; she cursed herself for her stupidity in marrying him, cursed Stephen for throwing her over so easily, cursed her first fiancé for causing the whole disastrous upheaval in her life.

But no ... Why blame others when the blame was hers entirely? Every person acted as he or she wanted to act, and not as others dictated. Apart from physical inducement, that was. Her actions had been her own at first; she alone had been responsible for them. Now, of course, she was subject to the will of her husband who, she knew without any doubt whatsoever, would not hesitate to use physical force to ensure that his desires were fulfilled or his orders obeyed.

A week passed and by now Raine had taken in the full precautions that were being put into operation in order to prevent her from running away from her husband. She was not allowed to go to the shops without Darius being with her; she was always under the eye of one or other of the gardeners whenever she walked in the grounds, and even a hairdresser was brought in rather than that she go into Delphi to visit the hairdresser there.

By the end of the week Raine was so furious that she decided to tackle her husband, even though she knew by painful experience that she would in all probability be reduced almost to tears by the sting of his tongue.

'Yes,' admitted Darius, 'you are being watched. What of it?' Arrogance in every word and gesture, and in the glance she received from those dark metallic eyes.

'The gardeners—what must they think, your employing them as prison guards!'

'They're very surprised that my wife might run from me, of course, but I strongly suspect they're finding the situation rather amusing. I don't pay them any extra, by the way.'

She was suddenly consumed by rage.

'I'm to be humiliated by servants, then?'

'Again you've asked for it. If I could trust you not to try to run away I'd call them off.'

She looked at him, her expression thoughtful, but still betraying the fury within her.

'If I give you my promise——?'

His laugh cut her short.

'We both know that such a promise would not be kept.'

She bit her lip, saw him nod his head, noticed the contempt appear in his eyes. She felt ashamed that he had so swiftly suspected her of deceit. And because of this feeling of shame she surprised herself as much as him by saying, a note of contrition in her voice,

'Yes, we both know it. I would never be able to keep such a promise simply because I shall always have the desire to escape from here.'

'The desire will fade with time, once you accept that its realisation will never come about.'

'I'm here for ever?'

'You are, my dear. Greeks hold what they have. I happen to have an exceptionally beautiful woman for a wife, and I intend to hold on to her.'

She glanced around. One of the gardeners was pottering about—ready to come on duty once his master had left her, decided Raine bitterly.

'I feel you're being rather over-optimistic,' she warned him at length. 'There must come a time when your vigilance will relax.'

Darius was shaking his head.

'It will never relax, Raine. It is you who are being over-optimistic.'

'It'll be like living in slavery!' she flashed, her temper flaring again.

'Call it what you wish,' he returned harshly. 'You should have thought of all this when you agreed to marry me.'

'You practically forced me into marriage!'

A sneer caught his mouth.

'You admitted in your note that you married me for revenge and what I could give you in the way of a settlement.'

She went red and turned away. What was the sense in all this argument? There was enough hostility between them without building up any more.

'If you want to do any shopping this afternoon,' Darius said, 'I am at liberty to take you.'

It would be a diversion, she thought.

'Yes, I would like to buy one or two necessities,' she returned.

'Immediately after lunch, then.'

He drove the big car into the town, and parked it near the museum. Raine desperately wanted an hour alone; she had always enjoyed shopping on her own, strolling around and window-gazing, taking her time. Always when she had been with someone else she had felt that she must hurry, and she was the same now, convinced that Darius would very soon become bored and in consequence his patience would run out. However, to her surprise he seemed content to wander with her, and he even passed an opinion over a present she wanted to buy for her sister. It was a silver filigree pendant on a fine silver chain. Raine had three different designs in front of her on the counter and she was having difficulty in making up her mind which one to choose. Darius stood looking over her shoulder for a moment or two, then picked one up and examined it.

After examining another he declared that the first one was beautifully made in comparison to the second. Encouraged by his comments, she asked him about the third one. He immediately shook his head.

'The design's too common,' he told her. 'One sees these by the thousands in Athens—and on most of the islands, for that matter.'

'I'll have this one, then,' she said, taking up the one he had said was beautifully made.

Surprising her again, he paid for it. She was undecided about allowing him to do so, seeing that it was a present from her to Drena. However, she said nothing, feeling she did not want to bring dissension into an atmosphere which was the friendliest since she had come to Greece. Not that it was really friendly; rather was it less hostile than usual.

'Would you care for a cup of tea or coffee?' asked Darius as they wandered towards a *caféneion* a few minutes later.

'Yes, I would.' This was his third surprise. She began to wonder what had mellowed him, and how long this mood would last.

They sat outside in the garden, under a gay umbrella. Darius ordered a small pot of tea for her and a Turkish coffee for himself. Raine wondered how he could drink the thick, black liquid, which was always served with a glass of water. But all Greeks drank it, and seemed to enjoy it.

They spoke little, each lost in thought. Raine's pensive gaze was fixed on the twin peaks of the Phaedriades —the Shining Ones—from whose wild ravine gushed forth the Castalian Spring, sacred to the cult of Apollo, and an important element in the function of the Delphic Oracle.

Suddenly Raine's attention was caught by the sharp and unexpected lift of her husband's head. He was looking beyond her and she instinctively twisted round to discover what had attracted his interest.

A golden blonde stood talking to the proprietor of the *caféneion* and, turning again, Raine saw that it was this girl at whom he was staring. She watched his changing expression, saw his eyes move swiftly to glance at his wife before his attention again became focused on the other girl. And then he was smiling; Raine gave a little gasp at the rapid transformation in his features. They had taken on so attractive a quality that it was difficult to believe he had ever reminded her of Satan himself. He rose from his seat and again Raine turned her head. The girl was approaching, having espied Darius sitting there, drinking his coffee.

'Marcella—how nice to see you. How long have you been back in Greece?'

'Only a couple of weeks.' The girl's eyes moved from Darius to Raine. 'We've rented a delightful villa just along the road here.'

Darius smiled and nodded, then introduced the two girls to one another.

'Your ... wife ...?' The girl seemed to withdraw, her smile fading slowly and a shadow entering her vivid blue eyes. 'I had no idea you were contemplating marriage, Darius.'

'It happened rather quickly,' he responded. 'You'll join us, Marcella?'

Marcella Cooper sat down without answering, but spoke immediately. Darius went off to find another chair.

'You must forgive me, Mrs Kallergis, if I seem a little surprised. You see, Darius was always the contented bachelor. We did not expect to find him with a wife.'

Raine managed a smile and merely said,

'Yes, I suppose his friends will be surprised.'

'You haven't met any of them yet? How long have you been married?' Marcella, crossing her elegant legs, casually opened her handbag and took out a slim gold cigarette case.

'Just less than a fortnight.'

Marcella stared at her, examining her face, her neck, her clothes. Under this rather haughty observation Raine felt herself colouring. She also felt her anger rising and hoped she would be able to control it.

'A fortnight, eh?' musingly and with a faint smile. 'You haven't got to know him very well, then?'

'I knew him in England,' answered Raine stiffly.

The girl's eyes flickered.

'How long were you acquainted with him in England?'

Raine cast her a haughty glance.

'Miss Cooper,' she said with quiet dignity, 'I'm not used to being questioned by strangers. I suggest you get my husband to satisfy your curiosity, when he comes back.'

If she expected the girl to be put out by this plain speaking she was mistaken. Marcella laughed mirthfully and said in a careless tone,

'I'm sorry if you took offence. Here in Greece we have no secrets from one another.' She idly tapped the end of her cigarette on the gold case, her amused gaze fixed on Raine's left hand, which was resting on the table. 'I have to admit that I'm intrigued by this marriage. It isn't like Darius to act in haste.'

'I expect he knew what he was doing,' returned Raine, and then, because her own curiosity was getting the better of her, 'You've known Darius for some time, evidently?'

Marcella nodded her golden head.

'My brother and I rented a villa here in Delphi over a year ago when we came into some money. Maurice—that's my brother—paints pictures, while I was acting as a guide for part of the time. We were both invited up to Darius's villa when he had a party one time.' The girl paused a moment. 'Darius and I became—er—very friendly, if you know what I mean?'

A frowning silence followed, as Raine scarcely knew how to deal with talk of this kind. It amazed her that any girl could speak in this way to someone she had met only a few moments previously. She said, changing the subject,

'Your brother paints, you say? Scenery?'

The girl nodded, pausing while she flicked a lighter and put it to her cigarette.

'Yes, mostly it's scenery——' She stopped and a dazzling smile was a prelude to the words, 'You were a long time, Darius. I feel guilty, taking your chair.'

'Not at all. What can I order for you?' he added, returning her smile. 'Here's the waiter now.'

He and Marcella had much to talk about and Raine found herself being ignored by them both. She felt indifferent about this treatment, being interested in what was going on around her. Men sitting about, playing cards and smoking numerous cigarettes. Some were just watching the card players, their fingers absently picking at their worry beads.

From a hillside came the tinkle of sheep bells, heard only when there was a pause in the *bouzouki* music coming from a tape recorder inside the café. From another direction was heard the cry of a donkey, shrill and complaining. Dominating everything was mighty Mount Parnassus with its spectacular crags—named Yambia and Nauplia by the peoples of ancient times —which gave the landscape of Delphi its singular and incomparable beauty.

Raine's attention was brought back to her husband again when she heard him mention her name.

'I have been telling Marcella how we met.' His voice was as cool and impersonal as ever; she wondered just what Marcella was thinking about their attitude towards one another—his indifference to the fact that his wife was not interested either in listening to his conversation with Marcella or in taking part in it.

'You have?' She raised her brows sceptically.

'At a party, yes.' She saw the sardonic smile at the corner of his mouth. It seemed to be a challenge and she felt tempted to tell the girl that they had met at the party given to celebrate the engagement beween herself and another man. What would he have to say then? Raine decided he would without difficulty manage to extricate himself from the situation into which she had deliberately put him.

'It must have been love at first sight,' commented Marcella, drawing strongly on her cigarette. Her blue eyes were amusedly concentrated on Raine's face, but she sensed the reciprocal amusement in Darius's gaze and she transferred her attention to him. Their eyes met, and held, and it seemed to Raine that there was a subtle message passing silently between her husband and this glamorous English girl who was obviously an old flame of his.

'Was it love at first sight, my dear?' There was no mistaking the sarcasm in Darius's voice, and Raine's kindled with anger.

'I can't truthfully say it was,' she returned after a tense little pause. 'I have never believed in such a possibility, Darius.'

'Oh, I don't know,' interposed Marcella. 'It has happened, time and time again.' Picking up her cup, she took a drink of the black coffee she had ordered. Darius, glancing at his wife's flushed face, must have decided that unless he changed the subject Raine might be tempted to say something which would embarrass him, for he asked Marcella why she and her brother had decided to return to Greece.

'We had no real ties in England, Darius, as you know. We went back because it was winter here and there was nothing doing. Maurice felt he should go home and sell some of his pictures there.'

'And did he sell some?'

'He sold them all; that's one reason why he wanted to come back.'

'To paint some more. Did he have an exhibition?'

'Yes, he had three as a matter of fact, and did exceptionally well with them all.'

'He's obviously going to make a name for himself.'

'He hopes to. The subjects here seem to have great appeal to people at home.' She drew on her cigarette again, then blew out the smoke, slowly, her eyes again meeting those of Darius. 'What time is it?' she inquired, mentioning that her watch had stopped and she could not get it going again.

'Ten minutes to four.'

'I must go. Shall we be seeing you some time soon?'

'You and Maurice must come to dinner. Would Friday be convenient for you?'

'Yes, of course. We're free agents, as you know.' Her dazzling smile flashed; Raine was forced to own that the girl was inordinately attractive, with her lovely hair and eyes, her slender figure and that air of smiling self-confidence. If she was an old flame of Darius's, then why had he given her up? Of course, Marcella might have given him up, but Raine doubted this.

She saw no reason why she should not question her husband about it, and this she did as they were sitting on the moonlit patio after dinner that same evening.

'So you've guessed we were more than friends,' he said blandly, ignoring her question for the time being. 'That was clever of you.'

She gave him a speaking glance.

'It wasn't clever at all. I'd have been an idiot had I not guessed it.' Her husband merely laughed and she added quietly, 'You haven't tried to deny it, then?'

'Why should I?' with all the old familiar arrogance.

'I wasn't married then, but in any case, I would please myself what I did.'

'You'd have an affair even though you were married?' she asked, diverted altogether now from the question she had asked.

'If I so wished, yes.' He glanced away, towards the wild crags that shone brilliantly in the moonlight. 'A man must have a diversion now and then.'

'This is the Greek male philosophy, I take it?'

'A world-wide philosophy. The difference is that in some parts of the world it's a secretive habit; in Greece we're more open, and honest.'

She made no response to this, and for a while silence fell between them, with only the whirring of the cicadas to prevent it from being a total silence. Palm trees, tall and still, stood outlined against the purple night sky, their long slender fronds forming lacy silhouettes which made patterns strange and weird. Raine listened to the cicadas, a sound which still fascinated her, although she knew she would become so used to it that she would not always notice it. Now, however, it was a part of the new environment and the new life that was hers. She was thrilled with Delphi, but she would never have admitted it to her husband. She was growing to love the people, but again she would not mention this to Darius. His home was the most beautiful she had ever seen; its setting was superb, with the mountains towering above, the hills where the sheep and goats grazed, watched by their black-robed shepherdesses who wandered among them with sphinx-like expressions on their sun-bitten faces. A hard life, but one without any real cares to blot out the peace that so many other people lacked. Contentment ran side by side with poverty, the joys of nature taking the place of the material things which money could buy. Raine felt she could live here quite happily, were her circumstances different from what they were. And she found herself envying Marcella, who seemed so free, so able to come and go as she liked, returning to Greece just whenever the fancy took her.

'You're very thoughtful.' Her husband's voice broke into her reverie and she glanced up. His face in the moonlight seemed a little less satanic than usual, but the leanness was more pronounced. His dark eyes were surveying her across the table and his voice was curt as he added, 'Where are you—with that insipid titled fop you were going to marry?' She said nothing and he went on, his voice harsh with contempt and his eyes raking her with arrogant dislike, 'You lost his money and the title—and you gained nothing.'

She looked at him angrily.

'Why couldn't you have left me alone? I was happy until you came into my life, and ruined it!'

'My dear girl, don't let's go into that again. Blame me if you must, but one day you're going to admit that the reason why you're unhappy at this moment is that you cheated.'

She gave a deep sigh, impatient with the conversation since it was totally unprofitable. She asked again which one of them it was who decided to make the break— Marcella or Darius himself.

'It was by mutual agreement,' he answered. 'That's how it should be. When two people discover they can no longer find enjoyment together then is the time to part.'

'You don't appear to consider it dishonourable to be admitting that Marcella was your pillow friend.' Raine looked curiously at him, saw him smile faintly before saying that Marcella did not mind in the least; everyone had known of the association; no one had shown any dislike of Marcella because of it.

'In my country these things are accepted,' he added, appearing to be sardonically amused by the expression on her face. 'It's a wonder that Marcella didn't tell you herself that we'd had that sort of relationship. It's just the kind of thing she would do,' he added with a faint smile of amusement.

'As a matter of fact, she did as much as tell me,' returned Raine, adopting an air of disgust which had not the slightest effect on her husband. 'I consider it the height of bad taste.'

'Which is only to be expected from a hypocrite like you,' he said with a sneer. 'It's time you took a good look at yourself, Raine. You might then not be so ready to look down upon others.'

She coloured.

'You prefer someone like Marcella?'

'I prefer honesty. You, my girl, have no idea what the word means, hence your inability to appreciate it in others.' His voice was a censure, as was his glance. Raine swallowed and looked away, to the towering ragged heights where, it was said, eagles nested. So remote ... Suddenly she wanted to be somewhere miles away from everyone—wanted to be alone. To be up there, in the mountains, must be wonderful. No people, no sounds but those of the breeze and perhaps a night bird's wings as it flew by in its search for food.

'I'm going in,' she said, turning to look at her husband. 'I'm tired.'

'It's early, but we'll turn in if that is what you want.'

She frowned at him.

'I want to be alone—just for once,' she said, impatience in her voice. 'I've not had a moment's privacy since coming here.'

'You won't have privacy at night,' he told her with a lift of his brows.

'Can't you sleep somewhere else for once!' She did not know what mischievous urge caused her to run so great a risk. Only when she saw his eyes kindle did she wish she had held her tongue.

'You're speaking to your husband,' he reminded her in a dangerously quiet tone.

'I'm tired,' she said in a low voice. 'I—I feel like being on my own ...' She was pleading now, and angry with herself for it. Yet she looked at him with the same plea in her eyes. To be alone would be heaven.

'You married me, Raine,' he said inexorably, 'and you now have to take the consequences. You're here to satisfy my desires, as I have already told you——'

'If that's all then why don't you get Marcella up here? She's that sort of a woman; I'm not!'

'You——!' He was white with fury; Raine, her heart banging against her ribs, wondered what had possessed her to act in so imprudent a manner. 'Get up!' he commanded. 'I said—get up!' But he reached for her wrist and brought her roughly to her feet.

'You're hurting me——'

'That's nothing to what you will get if you ever speak to me like that again!'

'Leave go of me!' she cried, twisting and struggling with every ounce of strength she possessed. 'I'm sick of your bullying! Does it not occur to you that I'm entitled to at least some respect?'

'Respect—you?' The contempt in his voice was as cutting as a razor's edge. 'Would you like me to give you a demonstration of the respect I have for you? Well, here it is!' And before she could begin to struggle again he had taken her face in his hand and was tilting it up. He bent his head and crushed her quivering

95

mouth beneath his own. There was neither respect in his kisses nor any vestige of gentleness. He let her go at length, but stood towering above her, his face twisted into almost evil lines. 'That's all the respect you'll get from me,' he told her harshly. 'And remember my warning—speak like that to me again and by God, you'll regret it!'

CHAPTER SIX

RAINE stood in the doorway of the dining-room, her pensive eyes wandering from the massive flower arrangements at either side of the window, to the glittering table with its crystal glass, its Sèvres china and its ornate candelabra, with matching cutlery and miniature wine coolers, four in all—one to the left of each cover—and each containing an exquisite flower arrangement of orchids and tiny green leaves.

Even the wealthy Redmaynes had never produced anything to surpass this—at least, not while she had known them. What a strange, unfathomable mixture her husband was! So primitive in many ways, his actions reflecting his pagan background, while in things like this—the preparation for the entertaining of his guests—he revealed the highest possible measure of elegance and good taste.

She stiffened suddenly and turned her head. Darius was at her side, his tall, immaculately-clad figure showing excellent taste in a very different way, the white topical suit cut to perfection so that it might have been moulded to his body. It contrasted with his bronzed skin, as did the white silk shirt with its inconspicuous trimming of very narrow broderie anglaise on the edge of the collar and down the front.

'Well,' he said, 'does this compare with what that pimp would have given you?'

Raine, pale but composed, turned her attention once more to the table.

'It compares,' was the stiff and cold reply she gave him.

'Favourably?'

She could not bring herself to give him praise.

'The two houses are so vastly different. The Redmaynes possess many beautiful heirlooms.'

'Like your engagement ring, for instance?' he returned sarcastically.

'That was a family heirloom, yes.' Automatically she glanced down at her left hand, recalling that Marcella had noticed the absence of an engagement ring. Her action, though slight, was caught by her husband, who immediately told her that his intention had been to buy her a ring when they were in Athens the day after their wedding. He had a friend there who would be able to produce stones of the highest quality.

'Your hurried departure on our wedding night naturally upset my plan. However, I shall see to the omission the next time I go to Athens.'

'I don't need an engagement ring,' she returned with a proud lift of her head.

'Nevertheless, you will have one.' Soft the tone, but implacable. It triggered off her anger.

'You can't force me to wear it, Darius!'

His black eyes narrowed; she twisted her head to escape his expression, but he took her chin in his firm grip and compelled her to face him.

'If I say you shall wear my ring, Raine, then you will wear it.' A pause, while her anger increased, causing a sudden tightening of the muscles in her throat. 'And now, just to illustrate my authority over you, I'm telling you to go and change your dress. Green doesn't suit you.' Releasing her chin, he allowed his eyes to wander over her slender figure, from the low-cut neckline of the evening dress to the hem with its tiny frill of ruched net.

She flared with temper.

'I shall *not* change my dress! I happen to like this one—and I *know* it suits me!'

'You'll change it,' he repeated in a dangerously quiet tone. 'And quickly. Our guests will be arriving within the next ten minutes or so.'

She was determined to make a stand. This domination could not go on for ever.

'I'm not changing it, Darius.' She was pale, and her heart was beating abnormally. One second she was telling herself that she was the sufferer in any stand she made against his arrogant authority, while the next second she was determined to fight that authority. 'I'm English, not a poor downtrodden Greek female who has had the spirit knocked out of her, leaving her humble and obedient.'

'I seem to have heard something like that before from you,' he reflected. 'It leaves me indifferent. English you might be, but you're now my wife, and much as it goes against your pride, you will obey me. Go and change your dress.'

So soft the voice, but invidiously threatening. Raine bit her lip as chagrin spread over her, and her eyes became bright with tears—tears of anger. Her thoughts flew to Stephen, and the life she could have enjoyed but for the unforeseen appearance of this man into her life. What a mess she was in! Surely there must be a way of escape. If she could defy him, and continue to do so, he might one day have had enough, and tell her to go. Even at the idea her heart seemed to lift with happiness. What a joy it would be to find herself in possession of her freedom! But the idea was fleeting. She was brought back to reality by her husband's imperious voice repeating his order that she should change her dress.

'I shan't——'

'Once again you've asked for it!' And on that he lifted her off her feet and carried her along the hall to the bedroom. There he set her down, went over to the wardrobe and took out another dress, an attractive creation in blue embroidered cotton. The neckline was high, the long full skirt gathered into a wide band at the waist. 'Put that on!' He threw it across a chair, then stood waiting, his height dominating the room.

'If—if I d-don't?' The fight had been taken out of her by his action in carrying her across the hall. She had begun to struggle, but desisted on seeing Katina emerge from the kitchen and stop dead in her tracks, a grin spreading over her chubby brown face. She would go back and relate the incident to Nicoleta, who in turn would probably repeat it to the two gardeners.

'If you don't,' repeated Darius with a warning lift of his brows, 'I shall be compelled to do it myself.'

She capitulated, snatching up the dress and disappearing into one of the side rooms. When she emerged he had gone, and something inside her seemed to snap. She would not wear it! A couple of minutes later she was again in the green dress.

She waited until she heard Marcella's voice before coming from the bedroom. Darius was in conversation with the girl and her brother and for a few seconds they did not notice Raine standing there, at the far end of the hall. She frowned at the way her husband was smiling at his visitors as he listened to something his old flame was saying, but she was examining his profile in a new light, wondering how he could effect these changes of mood so swiftly. Only a few minutes previously he had been haughty and officious, determined to domineer over her, yet here he was, all charm and geniality, the perfect host who, having gone to a great deal of trouble before the arrival of his two guests, intended that the dinner should be a complete success.

The moment arrived when Darius turned his head. An awful silence followed before, recovering himself, he performed his duty of introducing his wife to Marcella's brother. But his black eyes never left Raine's face and in their expression was a warning.

In response she gave him a small, triumphant smile. Whatever he had in mind for afterwards, when his friends had left, there was nothing he could do in the meantime.

But she was soon to learn just how little she knew of her husband.

'Shall we have drinks on the patio?' he invited, flicking a hand to indicate the door through which they would pass. 'Marcella, I know you will have your usual. And Maurice ...?'

'My usual too, Darius, please.' Maurice's grey eyes went to Raine. He had been interested in her from the moment of introduction, hardly able to take his eyes off her, although she guessed his real surprise had faded by now, his sister having told him of the meeting with Darius a few days ago.

'Raine, my dear? What shall I get for you?'

'A dry sherry, please.'

Darius smiled ... a strangely self-satisfied smile.

'Sherry it shall be.' Slow the words, and with a deliberation that was as incomprehensible as it was unnecessary ... or so it seemed to her at this moment.

He came out to where they had seated themselves on the patio, a small silver tray in his hand. After passing Marcella her drink he moved over to give Raine hers.

But he seemed to slip on something and the sherry went into her lap instead of finding its way to the table. Starting up at the shock of the cold liquid penetrating the thin material of her dress and filtering through to her flesh, she glowered at him with angry perception. He was all apology and concern.

'My dear ... I'm so sorry. Is it much? Yes, it is. You'll have to change your dress.' The black eyes had taken on an expression of sneering triumph. He was telling her that her own triumph had been short-lived, and that she could now go and do his bidding.

Her glance strayed to Marcella, and then to Maurice. Neither had noticed anything amiss; their faces registered slight concern, no more. It was an accident, they believed. Raine knew without any doubt at all that the spilling of the sherry had been deliberate.

If only she could find some way of paying him out, she thought as she went to the bedroom to change. His wrath was terrible to bear, but such was her desire to retaliate for actions such as this that she felt she would even go as far as enduring actual physical cruelty if only she could make his life unpleasant too.

Little did she guess that at least she was to have some diversion that evening, that her ego was to receive a booster—but then she had not counted on Maurice's interest stemming from anything other than that she had appeared so suddenly and unexpectedly on the scene—as the wife of the man who had been so interested in his sister.

But it was soon clear to Raine that Maurice was greatly attracted to her, although he did make some attempt to hide it. Darius, giving most of his attention to Marcella, failed to notice the glances which Maurice cast at Raine as they began their dinner.

The fish course was followed by a poultry course,

cooked Greek style, in wine, after which a soufflé was served and, finally, coffee and liqueurs were taken on the patio. It was well lighted this time, from lanterns hidden among the branches of the bougainvillaea vine that encircled the pillars set at intervals along the edge of the patio. But the moon was shining, sending a strange aura of unearthly violet light over the high massif of Mount Parnassus, giving it a sinister appearance.

Marcella was laughing as Darius held out her cigarette lighter for her. Raine caught Maurice's glance, saw him smile, as if he were feeling a deep sympathy for her. It was very plain that he considered her to be neglected, that he considered it deplorably wrong of Darius to give almost his whole attention to the girl who had at one time meant so much to him.

'More coffee, Mr Darius?' Nicoleta had appeared with a fresh pot of coffee. Darius nodded and the woman poured it out. The conversation became more general after that, but Raine soon began to suspect her husband of attempting to humiliate her in yet another way, and she became from then on keenly observant of his behaviour. She noted his quick turns of the head— towards Marcella. She saw his smiles, which were ready and always for the girl sitting beside him. But now and then, during this period of all-round conversation, he would send a covert glance in his wife's direction.

She at length grasped the situation. He was deliberately intending to humiliate her, Raine, by neglecting her when in the company of others.

The conviction was strengthened when, after the coffee things had been cleared away by Nicoleta, he said, glancing from Maurice to Raine,

'Marcella's just expressed the wish to take a short stroll. Do you mind if we leave you?'

Maurice's face was a study, while Raine, pale but dignified, forced a smile to her lips and replied in low, obliging tones,

'Of course not, Darius.'

'We'll not be too long away,' from Marcella lightly as she rose from her chair, assisted by Darius who gave her his hand.

Raine's eyes followed them until they became indistinct shadows mingling with the trees and bushes in the garden.

'I say ... I'm awfully sorry...' Awkwardly Maurice uttered the words, making an apology for something that was not his fault. 'You must be feeling dreadful.'

She brought her attention from the two shadows to the man sitting opposite to her. She noted his good-natured face, his light-brown hair and grey eyes set wide apart below curving eyebrows that were almost bushy, and meeting across the bridge of his nose. His hands rested on the table—the long slender hands of an artist, and his fingers fidgeted as she watched. He was uncomfortable to say the least, and she had a sudden urge to put his mind at rest.

'It's nothing of importance, Maurice. I have you for company. Would you like a drink of something?'

He shook his head, relief taking the place of his former anxiety.

'It's nice of you to take it like this. My sister hinted that she'd not made any secret of her past friendship with Darius.'

'No, she said enough for me to guess she'd been his girl-friend.'

'Someone would have told you eventually,' he said. 'It was known and accepted; they're like that in this country.' He looked curiously at her, a certain hesitancy about him. But soon he was saying, as if he could not stop himself, 'I don't know how Darius can treat you like this, Raine. You're so beautiful—I'd have expected him to have eyes for no one else.'

'We live in modern times,' she returned with a laugh.

'You yourself—I mean, you're so trusting. It would be more understandable if you weren't, seeing that you know about their past friendship.' She said nothing and he added, almost to himself, 'It's said that there can be no love without trust, so it's natural, I suppose, that you trust your husband.' He sounded doubtful, though, and again Raine laughed. She found the situation amusing, and wondered what this nice young man would have to say were she to confess what was in her mind: that she hoped Darius would make love to Marcella, for then he would leave his wife alone. Thinking about this possibility, Raine found herself hoping that the affair which was terminated by mutual agreement would ripen again and that the couple would take up where they had left off. Surely Darius would then decide to end his marriage.

'My husband mentioned that they had agreed to part, so obviously there was no animosity between them. This being the case, they're still friends, aren't they? One cannot expect them to ignore one another. I accepted the position when Darius invited Marcella to dine here tonight.'

He had begun to frown even before she had finished speaking.

'There's some mystery,' he said with sudden decision. 'How long did you know Darius before you married him?'

'Not very long, why?'

'Because no one expected him to marry a foreigner. In fact, none of his friends and acquaintances expected him to marry for some time yet!'

Raine paused, her eyes wandering to the mountain. Above the rocky crags an eagle glided in the moonlight, like a shadow in the sky.

At length she said, curiosity getting the better of her,

'It was strange that Darius and Marcella parted like that. They seem so suited to one another, and obviously they are able to entertain one another.'

'You have no idea why they parted?'

She shook her head.

'None whatever.'

Again he was hesitant.

'I don't know if I ought to tell you.' His tone was strange and she looked swiftly at him.

'It wasn't just that they became tired of one another —in that particular way, I mean?' She thought of what she was saying and wondered if any other new bride had ever carried on such a discussion before. Her thoughts were reflected in her companion's next words.

'You're so calm about this whole thing, Raine. One would almost believe that you hadn't married Darius for love—I mean, such marriages do take place, don't they?'

She merely smiled at this and said,

'You haven't answered my question, Maurice.'

'No, I haven't. And I don't think it would be very mannerly of me if I did. It's the sort of thing a woman like to keep secret.'

Raine's curiosity increased by leaps and bounds as she heard this.

'You ought not to get this far and then stop,' she chided. 'I just can't contain myself. I must know the rest.'

'My sister would not thank me for telling you the reason why she and Darius parted.'

Raine frowned, racking her brain to find the answer herself. They had parted by mutual agreement, yet were still friends. The parting had occurred owing to something which Marcella wanted to keep secret. She shook her head in bewilderment, glancing at Maurice and saying,

'This secret you mention—if it had not been there, would Marcella and Darius have married, do you think?'

He gasped at her calm composure, at the almost impersonal manner in which she could ask a question like that.

'There *is* some mystery about your marriage, isn't there, Raine?' He was pleading all at once and she saw with swift perception that he had allowed hope to rise within him—hope that a friendship might develop between Raine and himself.

Raine's mind became absorbed by her husband's treatment of her, not only when they were alone, which was often unbearable enough, but now, when he had gone off with his old flame, uncaring that she might be dreadfully embarrassed, that she might be sitting awkwardly opposite to Maurice, squirming at what he must be thinking. Well, she was not squirming, nor was she feeling in any way awkward. Quite the contrary, in fact. She was happier at this moment than at any other time since coming to Greece. She had met someone who liked her.

A friendship between her and Maurice? If only it had been possible. They were both lonely; they had already, in one short evening, found an easy relationship which had allowed a conversation that was almost intimate.

'Yes,' she said decisively at last, 'there is a mystery about my marriage to Darius.'

His grey eyes flickered.

'You'll tell me about it?'

She paused, aware that she owed no loyalty to the man who had wrecked her life, yet for some uncomprehensible reason averse to making *his* life an open book.

'No, Maurice,' she said apologetically at last. 'I can't tell you about it.'

'But you're not in love with him, and he's not in love with you?'

Again she paused. But then she realised it would be futile to tell a lie, even if she wanted to, which she did not.

'It's obvious, I suppose,' was all she said in reply, and she saw him nod.

'I knew it instinctively, and yet I could not bring myself to believe that any man could be married to a lovely girl like you and not be in love with her.'

She coloured daintily, turning her head away so that he should not see.

'This secret,' she ventured presently. 'I asked you if Marcella and Darius would have married had not this secret existed.'

Maurice was a moment or two in thought before he replied,

'Yes, Raine. It's my belief that they were ideally suited, and had other things been all right, then they would have married.'

'Other things,' she repeated musingly. The girl wasn't already married, for had this been the case Maurice would surely have said so. In any case, marriages these days could always be dissolved. She looked across at him, saw the firm line of his jaw and knew he would not proffer any further information on this particular subject. At least, not yet. Later, perhaps, when he and she had got to know one another a little better. 'You said just now that you would not have expected Darius to marry a foreigner. But your sister is English?' she pointed out.

'After they had parted Darius told someone he was not looking any further than Greece for a wife. He also said, though, that he was in no particular hurry to get married.'

'If they were ideally suited, and in love, then how could they part so easily?'

'That's something I've never understood, Raine,' he admitted, a slight frown settling on his forehead. 'I was puzzled myself about the whole thing, because Marcella seemed not to mind about the break.'

'In that case,' persisted Raine, 'they weren't in love with one another?'

'No, I suppose one must draw that conclusion.'

'Yet you believe they would have married—but for this secret of Marcella's.'

'I do believe they'd have married. I believe they had a most satisfactory relationship——'

'Satisfactory, or satisfying?' interrupted Raine with a little smile.

'You're very outspoken,' he said, but with a responsive smile.

'This is an outspoken conversation,' she replied. 'I've never been so free with anyone in so short a time before —at least, not that I can remember.'

'Nor have I.' His voice took on an eagerness which made her feel good. She had been despised so long, treated with derision and the deepest contempt, that Maurice's interest and admiration were balm to her unhappiness. She wished she had some freedom, so that a friendship could develop between Maurice and herself—a platonic friendship, of course. They could have met now and then, just for a chat. A sigh escaped her as she was forced to own that this was quite impossible.

'Tell me about yourself?' she invited, deciding it was time the subject was changed. 'Your sister told me you paint pictures.'

'Yes, that's right. I come here because the scenery is what appeals to me. As it seems to appeal to my prospective customers back home, the arrangement's most satisfactory.'

'I love the scenery here too. I've never lived in so beautiful and spectacular a place.'

'You've been to the Sanctuary, of course?'

Raine shook her head. How could she tell him that she was never allowed out alone?

'No, I haven't.'

'Hasn't Darius offered to take you yet?' he asked in surprise. 'The people who live here in Delphi are so proud of the Sanctuary that they invariably show a great eagerness to take visitors round—not that you're a visitor,' he added unnecessarily. A moment's pause ensued and then, 'Look, Raine, can I take you over the site some time?'

She bit her lip hard. So acceptable an offer, it was. Nice company, with a man she felt sure she could trust ... and she could not go with him because she was a prisoner in her husband's home.

'I'm sorry, Maurice,' she said flatly, 'but I can't go with you.'

He frowned in puzzlement.

'Darius won't mind, surely? After all, if he can go off like this with Marcella then how can he object to your taking a trip with me to the Sanctuary?'

'None ... really ...' If only she could find a way of outwitting her husband over the matter of her freedom! The very idea of having to refuse Maurice's invitation was so galling that she could have cried with frustration.

'Well then, perhaps we can make a definite date?' His eyes wandered as he heard a slight sound coming from the direction of the garden. 'They're returning,' he said. 'We'll mention it to Darius——'

'No,' she interrupted, far too hastily, and Maurice looked at her in puzzlement. 'He—he doesn't like me going out on my own, Maurice.'

'You won't be on your own, you'll be with me.'

'Yes—but——' She stopped, fury rising within her at this state of helplessness in which she found herself. 'I can't go with you, that's all I have to say.'

His puzzlement increased; he ignored the finality in her voice and murmured curiously,

'You'd like to come with me, wouldn't you, Raine?' She made no answer and he continued, 'I know you would. I also sense an anger about you, as though you're resenting having to refuse me.'

She nodded unhappily, and for one fleeting moment she could have confided in him, so desirous was she for sympathy.

'I can't come with you; it's impossible for me to get away,' she told him at last.

'Impossible, Raine? But you're not a prisoner ...' His voice trailed away to silence as the other two came into clear view on approaching the patio.

'Did you have a pleasant stroll?' Raine did not know whether or not she was glad of their return. She felt that had she and Maurice had more time together she would have given in to her desire and told him everything. On the other hand, however, her pride rejected the idea of making a confidant of a man she had met for the first time only a few hours ago.

'Most pleasant,' answered Darius with a glance which

moved from his wife's slightly flushed face to the frowning, puzzled countenance of Marcella's brother. 'Have you two had a pleasant chat?'

Maurice looked at him with a hard expression.

'Delightful,' he answered. 'Raine was asking me about my painting—a subject which, being so important to me, was naturally one which I was more than willing to discuss with her.'

She threw him a glance. It said a great deal ... and it sowed the seed of friendship between them, although how this was to grow and blossom in such adverse circumstances was, to Raine's mind, a near impossibility.

CHAPTER SEVEN

DARIUS came into the bedroom just as Raine was brushing her hair. Their eyes met through the mirror, but Raine soon lowered her lashes. She was feeling hopeless, as if there was no light in her life, nor would there ever be light again. The depression had dropped over her like a cloak immediately their guests had departed, shortly after midnight, for she knew without any doubt at all that she wanted a friendship to develop between Maurice and herself. She liked his open face and his smile. He was intelligent, had an interesting occupation; he was smart in his dress, and he was spotlessly clean. Added to this, he had shown that he liked her and she was certain that he too would welcome the idea of a friendship developing between them.

But how? This man standing there, arrogance oozing from him, accentuated by the proud set of his shoulders, his haughty expression, and even the dressing-gown he wore, with its snarling dragons breathing fire from their nostrils, held her prisoner.

'You are beautiful enough ...' Soft words reaching her; a hand taking her wrist and the other imperiously removing the hairbrush and placing it—with what to Raine seemed to be exaggerated deliberation—on the dressing-table. She was drawn to her feet, half inclined to resist, to snap out the words,

'Leave me alone!' but she remained speechless, rising meekly and, without protest, allowing her face to be lifted by his fingers under her chin. Darius bent his dark head and she braced herself for the feel of his lips on hers.

'Yes, you are certainly beautiful...' His hand took hold of a few strands of her hair; he held them for a moment in silent contemplation before letting them run through his fingers and fall on to her shoulder. His dark eyes moved, devouring her delectable curves with all the arrogance of possession. She coloured, seething inside her, yet so calm a veneer did she maintain that he produced a triumphant little smile and said, in that hateful voice of sardonic amusement, 'It would seem, my wife, that I have brought you to heel.'

She looked at him through eyes that were as cool as the tone she used,

'You sound most confident, Darius.'

She felt his hand move, to her neck. His fingers began to encircle it and she shivered.

'I'll not strangle you,' he laughed, yet the long lean fingers did tighten a little. 'I would hate not to be able to make this heart of yours quicken with anticipation.' His hand now moved to her breast; she flinched, yet within seconds she was calm again. But the calmness was no more than defiance, an attempt to prove to him that she could remain aloof to his magnetism. He laughed, a low and half-amused chuckle, and brought her close to his body. She felt his hand on the back of her head, forcing her lips to his. 'Wretch!' he exclaimed when she failed to reciprocate. 'So I haven't quite brought you to heel, after all.' So close his mouth to her cheek, so ardent his body near to hers. 'But I don't really think I want complete surrender at this stage. No conqueror ever wanted to win without a fight. There would be little or no satisfaction in such a conquest.'

His mouth caressed her cheek, while with one hand he untied the dainty little bow which secured her negligée at the waist. The garment eventually fell to the ground, leaving Raine clad in a diaphanous nightgown of white nylon and lace. Darius held her from him and allowed his ardent eyes to take their fill of her beauty. She closed her eyes, her thoughts flitting about chaotically as, one moment, she wanted to attempt an escape, and another moment she was telling herself that her pride would suffer, since her husband's strength would soon conquer hers. Then she would be in an even more humiliating position than she was at present.

But what she was really trying to combat was the power of his attraction as a man ... a man who was her husband. She recalled with startling clarity those moments on the verandah of her fiancé's home when this Greek had tempted her, bringing her to that state of half-expectancy which had caused her such shame later, when she allowed her mind to dwell upon it. Then in the caravan, when, after the interruption that had saved her from total surrender, he had implied that she, as well as he, had not found the interruption welcome.

Darius was speaking, breaking into her reverie.

'Open these lovely eyes and look at me.' His voice was a command which seemed to snap something within her and she twisted right out of his arms.

'Is that the way you spoke to Marcella?' she fumed. 'Giving orders as if you were some sort of a god?'

The black eyes kindled, though the faintly accented voice was calm,

'Shall we leave Marcella out of it? You have taken her place, but that does not mean that either my behaviour or yours must follow the pattern that hers and mine did. We are *us*; we shall think and act as our own wills lead us.'

Raine's brows shot up at this.

'Have I any free will of my own, Darius?'

'In a way, you have,' he returned unexpectedly. 'You come to me of your own free will——'

'Where, might I ask, did you get that idea?' she flashed. 'Such a statement's absurd!'

To her surprise he only laughed.

'How you love to deceive yourself, Raine. Yet, deep down inside you, the truth shouts out, even though you make a tremendous effort to suppress it.' He paused, regarding her with a quizzical stare. 'Well, aren't you going to ask about this truth I've mentioned?'

She shook her head.

'I just don't know what you mean, Darius. None of it makes the slightest sense to me.'

'Liar,' he accused softly. 'And you're a shirker too—shirking an answer. Well, I shall give you the answer all the same. I once told you that I attract you just as much as you attract me.' He looked straightly at her, a challenge in his dark metallic eyes. To his intense satisfaction hers were lowered after a few seconds of this scrutiny. 'You try to deny even to yourself that this is true, but you're fooling neither of us by pretending that you dislike my lovemaking——'

'I'm not pretending!'

He looked at her across the room.

'I forgot, didn't I,' he said contemptuously, 'that honesty is not a trait which you possess?'

She coloured hotly, conscious of his glance of distaste. It riled her that he was so perceptive—and yet it was not surprising that he knew of the strength of his power over her; she had far too much difficulty in resisting him ... and she more often than not failed utterly to do so.

Her eyes wandered to her negligée. She wished she could reach it, but it was lying at his feet. She felt so vulnerable, standing here, with his eyes insolently raking her figure—assessing it in terms of pleasure, she did not doubt, since this sort of thing came natural to the Greek male. Presently she had to say,

'Will you give me back my negligée, please?'

He raised his straight black brows a fraction.

'You'll not be needing that, my dear.'

She swallowed the hard little lump in her throat, thinking of Marcella and wishing with all her heart that the affair between her and Darius had never ended. 'I would like it, Darius.' She had no idea how young she sounded, and how helpless. His eyes flickered with a strange expression and then, to her complete astonishment, he stooped, picked up the dainty garment and passed it to her. But before she had time to put it on he had taken her in his arms and, crushing her to him, he sought her lips in a kiss that seemed even more passionate than any that had gone before. She closed her eyes, her mind incapable of clear thoughts as, carried on the tide of his ardour, she surrendered to the demand of those sensuous lips. He was triumphant, she knew, and yet she could not gather the strength to resist the overmastering desire he was deliberately creating in her. Her body seemed to flow with warmth, and her heart, so close to his breast, was thudding so loudly that she could actually hear it. A deluge of longing swept through her and when her husband said, with a low triumphant laugh,

'Do you still want this thing?' she shook her head, and answered in husky, quivering tones, dropping the negligée on to the floor,

'N-no, Darius—I d-don't want it.'

He laughed again, a little louder this time.

'I knew I'd conquer you, my girl! And I shall always do so—just whenever I like!' And with that he swept her slender body up into his arms and the next moment the room was plunged into darkness.

Dawn was stealing the purple from the sky when Raine awakened. A turn of her head and her eyes beheld her husband, sleeping so peacefully, his breathing even, the bedcovers moving rhythmically up and down.

Filled with shame and anger at her own weakness, she rose swiftly and after bathing and dressing she went out on to the balcony. The massif of Mount Parnassus shone crimson in the glow of morning; shapes on the foothills to the left moved slowly—figures of animals and men from the mystic tales of the Bible. A shepherd with his sheep and goats, his staff standing out sharp-edged against the shadowed slopes that formed the backcloth for this pastoral scene. So peaceful, so silent —but within Raine's heart a great tumult. Questions flittered through her mind, questions that she could not ignore. Was she no better than one of his other pillow friends, a wanton whose desires were more important than her ideals? Undoubtedly her husband excited her, aroused in her instincts which, because she did not love him, were, to her, base, to say the least. She thought of her first love, the fiancé who had let her down. It was owing to her high ideals that she could not condone such conduct. Had she been able to do so then she would now be married to a man whom she loved. But would she? He might by now have killed her love by failing her again and again.

Her reflections were brought to an abrupt end by a sound behind her. Darius had risen, had donned his dressing-gown and was coming out to stand beside her on the balcony. She turned, slanting him a glance. In profile he was just as forbidding as seen in full face, and yet he was handsome too, in that firm strong way which appealed to so many women. He was a man apart, no doubt about that, a man with tremendous strength of character, of dominance and, she felt sure, a man of the greatest dependability.

He looked down into her face, his prolonged unsmiling stare disconcerting in that it was incomprehensible. What was he thinking? Probably of last night when, tempted by the draw of his magnetism, she gave herself not only willingly, but joyfully as well.

A victory for him, but by no means the first ... although it was probably the greatest. If she had loved him, she thought, and he loved her, then life could be bliss.

Love! It was not to be thought of in connection with the man who had ruined her life. Even Stephen would never have had love from her—and she strongly suspected that he knew it and did not mind in the least— nor would she have ever had love from him. He wanted a beautiful picture to enhance his home, to be admired by his guests; she had wanted security and an above average home. The title had come as a bonus, but a welcome one for all that.

This husband of hers was solely responsible for her loss, and if she lived with him for fifty years she could never come to love him.

'What are you thinking about?' His quiet, faintly accented voice held curiosity, nothing else.

'Things,' she replied, sorting out in her mind what she would tell him, should he persist in asking questions.

'What things?'

'My life before you came into it.'

'Tell me about your life,' he invited, moving a little so that he could sit on the wide teak rail of the balcony. 'What did you do before you got yourself engaged to that fop I found you with?'

If it was his intention to rile her he succeeded. She

coloured angrily, and her brown eyes held a glitter of ice as she returned,

'I'd have you know that Stephen was a respected member of the English nobility. I'd have been a countess but for you!'

'Yes,' he mused, deliberating on this for a while. 'I somehow cannot imagine you in that role at all.'

'Why not? Are you suggesting I'd be out of my depth?'

'Oh, no. I'm suggesting nothing of the kind. But I can't see you being for ever on your dignity, or dressing up to attend some boring function or the wedding of some simpering debutante and her dandified bridegroom. Much less can I see you going around opening bazaars and garden fêtes, receiving bouquets from tiny tots with scrubbed faces and runny noses.' He stopped, because she had begun to laugh. 'You look wonderful,' he said with the most odd inflection. 'Do you realise, Raine, that this is the first time I've seen you laugh?'

She nodded reflectively, lifting her eyes to examine his face. A certain relaxing of the muscles had brought a softer quality to his features, and something strange stirred within her. It brought back vivid recollections of last night, especially when, his passion stilled, he had lain beside her, one arm round her waist. She had not wanted to move, nor did she want him to move either. They had both slept in this position.

He was now waiting for her to say something. She searched for a cutting retort, but instead found herself saying, in a rather flat little voice,

'I haven't had much to laugh about recently, Darius.'

The black eyes flickered. He said smoothly,

'Your life might not be so bad if you will make up your mind to accept my word as law and not to argue with me as is your habit.'

'I'm to remember, always, that you are in authority over me?' Her voice did contain a little tartness now.

'If that is the way you prefer to describe it, then yes, you must remember that I am in authority over you.'

'If we could reach a state of equality——?' She stopped, amazed by what she was saying. She had no desire to enter into a state of friendship with him, which was what she had been about to imply. He too must have known what she would have said had she finished her sentence, for he gave her a sardonic smile and said,

'If we could reach a state of equality we might get along fairly well together?' He shook his head. 'Nothing doing, Raine. You've cheated and you'll pay, as I've already said. There will be no equality for you—ever.'

'You keep reminding me about my cheating, but what of your conduct?'

'I saved you from a disastrous marriage,' was his bland rejoinder. 'You'd have been bored with that life within a month.'

'I'd have found something to do.'

'Such as?'

'Oh ... I could have learned to play golf——'

'Golf! Good lord, girl, do you know what you're saying? You'd learn to play golf in order to combat the boredom of your marriage?'

She blushed. It did sound ridiculous when put like that.

'I wouldn't have been as bored as you imagine,' she told him defensively after a pause. 'There's plenty to do if you have money.'

Impatiently he sighed, and changed the subject.

'I asked about your life before you met him,' he reminded her. 'Tell me about your home. You've no parents; I did learn that much.'

'Yes, and you knew that I worked in an office and had my own flat.'

'I came there, if you remember,' he returned in some amusement.

She let that pass without comment, going on to tell him a little of her parents' attitude towards their two daughters.

'They should never have had children,' she ended, and a hint of sadness and regret had entered her voice.

Darius moved on his not very comfortable seat, settling himself more firmly on it.

'So it would seem,' he agreed. 'They appeared to be totally absorbed in one another.'

'They were.'

'It was fortunate that they did have two children. I would have expected them to stop at one.'

'Drena and I always believed we were both accidents.' So casual her tone as she said this. He seemed amused, but only faintly. As a matter of fact, his face had taken on a rather grim expression, which was reflected in his tone of voice when he spoke.

'This lack of love in childhood might just be the cause of the way you are now—— No, don't take offence and flare up at me, for I can assure you you'll come off worse than I in a battle of words. As I was saying, the things you missed as a child could very well have been the direct cause of your being unable to fall in love——'

'I'm not unable to fall in love,' she interrupted, quite without thought. 'I was once engaged to someone else. It was a love match.'

He frowned in inquiry.

'What happened?'

She hesitated, vexed with herself for revealing this circumstance of her past life. However, as she saw from her husband's expression that he would insist on an answer, she told him what had taken place.

'He obviously preferred the other girl at that particular time,' she went on, 'so I gave him up.'

'He wanted to marry you, though?'

Raine nodded.

'Yes, he did. It was only a diversion, he said, and there was no love between him and this other girl.' As she spoke her voice became low and husky, the result of a recurrence of the emotion which had enveloped her at that time. Her husband remained silent, watching her intently, his face a mask, unreadable and severe. 'I did not want to break the engagement, but I felt he might let me down again—after we were married, perhaps.'

'Perhaps?' with a lift of his eyebrows. 'Most certainly he would have let you down. You were very wise to throw him over.'

She looked swiftly at him, then said slowly,

'You do not believe in infidelity?'

The dark eyes seemed to blaze, with indignation.

'Certainly not!'

'You yourself would be faithful to your wife?'

Faintly he smiled now and answered,

'Only if my wife and I were in love with one another. This is what I meant. If, like you and me, there is no love, but it's merely a marriage of convenience, with you wanting wealth and me desiring your beauty, then of course I owe you nothing in the way of fidelity.' So emphasised the tone, so direct the look he gave her. Raine was impelled to retaliate by saying,

'So I also am not bound by fidelity?'

Darius came down from his perch, and stood over her, a towering menacing figure with features that had undergone the most rapid and dramatic transformation. He looked like Satan himself, she thought, backing away until she felt the rail against her shoulders.

'You, wife, owe me total fidelity! It would be fatal for you to let me down in that way ... because I'd not hesitate to strangle you!' And with that he turned and re-entered the bedroom.

Raine, white to the lips, twisted round and stared out across the gorge to the mountain, and again she was struck with its peacefulness. The shepherd was still there, and another was climbing slowly up the hillside. She thought of the Sanctuary, and of Maurice's invitation to take her there.

'I must have some freedom,' she whispered, almost hysterically, 'or I shall go mad! I'll make Darius a solemn promise not to try to escape...'

She put a brake on these thoughts, for she knew she would never keep such a promise; she would not be able to, as escape was ever the dominating idea of her mind.

And if she had no intention of keeping the promise, then she would never make it.

CHAPTER EIGHT

It was only to be expected that the atmosphere between Raine and her husband would grow oppressive with tension. Darius's ruthless, tyrannical attitude towards Raine seemed at times to be forced, and yet it continued mercilessly, as if he must constantly remind her of what she had done. She in turn would revile him for coming into her life and deliberately breaking up her engagement to Stephen.

'I saved you from a disastrous marriage,' he would invariably answer, his black eyes filled with contempt as they swept over her from head to foot.

'What was it to you that I might make a disastrous marriage?'

'After I met you, it meant a great deal. I knew I wanted you for my own.'

'A man of honour would have resigned himself to the fact that I had already found the man of my choice.'

A sneer curved his hard lips.

'The life of your choice,' he corrected with contempt. 'The man could have been a dwarf for all you'd have cared. It was his bank balance in which you were interested, not the man himself.'

She coloured; put the way her husband put it, her conduct sounded utterly contemptible, so much so that she squirmed inside, feeling debased.

'I had decided to marry for money simply because I'd been let down previously.'

'A thoroughly weak excuse for your behaviour,' he said. 'I have no time for self-pity.'

She managed to lift her eyes to his, aware that her colour was still heightened. Why should this pagan Greek be able to make her feel so ashamed of herself that all she really wanted to do was hang her head? Fury rose within her, but for some indefinable reason she kept it well hidden.

'It's not a question of self-pity,' she denied. 'I was hurt by my fiancé, and disillusioned. I had no intention of going through that sort of anguish again, so I decided to marry for money. After all,' she added on a derisive note, 'love doesn't last.'

Her husband's expression underwent a dramatic change, and Raine gained the extraordinary idea that it was on the tip of his tongue to deny this, to state emphatically that love could last, if those concerned wished it to, that was. However, all he said was,

'You're not unique in that you've been disillusioned. Nevertheless, you decided you were more badly done to than others who had undergone similar experiences and so you became obsessed by the desire for revenge.' He stopped, to throw her a glance of contempt. 'It didn't matter to you who was the object of that revenge——'

'Stephen was satisfied with the bargain,' she broke in shortly. 'You're wrong in concluding that he was the object of my revenge.'

The dark eyes raked her with dislike.

'What are you trying to do?—vindicate yourself?'

She coloured again.

'My actions at that time had nothing whatsoever to do with you,' she retorted, feeling inferior beside his calm assurance, his judicial manner, his condemnation.

'Later,' he said musingly, and bypassing the words she had just uttered, 'I became the object of your revenge.'

'It was your own fault!'

'But now, my lovely wife, you are the object of *my* revenge.' His words had slowed down and she caught her breath. She was fully prepared for what was coming next. The black eyes, triumphantly taking in the resignation that had entered hers, held a trace of sardonic amusement in their depths. 'Come here,' he commanded softly, and pointed imperiously to a spot close to where he was standing. 'So ... your chin goes up and you are intending to begin an argument. My advice is—don't, Raine; I assure you that, as always, you will in the end succumb to my superiority.'

Tears of mortification welled up in her eyes. She could fight him, yes, but as he said, she would in the end be forced into total submission by his superior strength. She shrugged, then moved obediently forward, every nerve rebelling at the idea that he could humiliate her so.

He took her face in his hand, held it while he stared fixedly into her eyes. Then he bent his head and she steeled herself for the contact of his hard demanding mouth on hers. She stood passively, while his arms encircled her slender body, and his lips possessed hers with almost frightening ardour. He drew away, looking down at lips that were quivering in slow, convulsive movements.

'What an enticing little witch you are!' He swept her to him again, his kisses reflecting the fire which was racing through his veins as they moved from her lips to her throat and then to her shoulder. Raine was no longer passive against the lithe hardness of his body. The warmth of her desire was spreading through her; the secret confession within her was that she would not resist him, even had she possessed the strength to do so.

However, moments like these were rare; in the main,

she made a tremendous effort to retain a coldness towards him, an unresponsiveness which infuriated him even while it acted as fuel to the fire within him, and invariably his wife suffered for what he termed her obstinacy. Life for her would be more comfortable if only she would accept her fate, resigning herself to the life that was hers from now on.

'I shall never become resigned!' she had flashed one day when, even yet again, he had proffered her this 'good advice' as he described it. 'There will surely come a time when your vigilance will weaken—when one of those gaolers you've set to watch my every movement will be off guard. Then, Darius, you can be sure I shall seize the opportunity of escape.'

'It is more than their lives are worth to be off guard,' he returned smoothly. Then he added, a hint of admiration entering his voice for the very first time, 'I commend your honesty, my dear. I must admit that I've been expecting you to approach me with promises not to escape if only I will call the guard off.'

She looked at him, pale and composed, her eyes meeting his in a clear and direct glance.

'I did say, if you remember, that I would never promise anything unless I could keep that promise.'

'Which makes you a contradictory character.'

Her eyes flashed.

'I don't see how you've reached a conclusion like that!'

His dark eyes flickered.

'The honesty does not line up with the avariciousness you displayed in marrying me for the settlement I could make.'

Raine said, scarcely knowing why she should be so venturesome,

'You're fiendishly annoyed with yourself for being duped, aren't you?'

'I'm certainly not pleased with myself for being so trusting.' Smooth the tone, but Raine could detect the sudden fury contained in it. The superior and lordly Darius Kallergis being duped by a mere female! The idea would rankle for years, she thought.

'You ought to have suspected that I'd seek for revenge.'

He looked away and, strangely, she gained the impression that he was swallowing something hard that had settled in his throat. However, his voice was as harsh as ever she had heard it when eventually he spoke.

'A lot of good it's done you. I'll wager you've never regretted anything so much in the whole of your life.' There was an evil twist to his mouth, a satanic glint in his eyes. 'You met your match in me,' he went on in a jeering, triumphant voice. 'But I haven't finished with you yet. I said you'd pay dear for your trickery, and I meant it.'

Still pale, but not quite so composed as she was, Raine looked at him and said,

'Make the most of your present opportunities, Darius, because I can assure you I shall make my escape one day.'

He was shaking his head even before she had finished speaking.

'Escape will be impossible. What I have I hold, Raine. You have already learned about my very possessive nature.'

Scenes like this occurred over and over again, with the very natural result that the animosity existing between them increased. Raine, aware that this life could not continue, found that every waking moment was concentrated on getting away from this pagan who was her husband. But success was never even within sight.

'It seems so utterly hopeless,' she cried, pacing her bedroom as she had paced it so many times before. 'I've no money, no means of transport—and in any case, I'd never even be able to get away from the grounds of this house!'

She inquired one day whether he was intending to have her meet his friends. He shook his head instantly.

'Too risky,' he said. 'My best friends are married to English girls. I would not have you meet them, and whisper urgently that you were being kept a prisoner.'

Her interest was revealed in the sudden widening of her eyes. She said, bypassing his last sentence,

'Your friends are married to English girls? Did they meet them here, or in England?'

'Here.' He seemed amused all at once. 'They certainly weren't abducted,' he laughed. 'They came willingly.'

'In which case,' retorted Raine, 'they obviously had not been molested as I was!'

He allowed that to pass, and within seconds he had walked away, striding towards the house while Raine, standing on the lawn where they had been talking, watched him, admitting to the impressive majesty of his bearing, the easy way he walked, like an athlete, the wide noble shoulders and proud carriage of the head, its black hair gleaming in the sun, clean and faintly waved. The sudden catch of a pulse told her that she ought to examine her own feelings at this time, as she allowed her pensive gaze to remain on his figure as with each stride the distance between her and Darius lengthened.

Examine her own feelings ...

What was there to examine? She was vitally aware

already of the futility of the continually recurring wish for freedom. She had only to turn her head at this moment to be sure of being carefully watched. Not only was one of the gardeners in evidence, but, at the far end of the orchard, Nicoleta could be seen, sweeping leaves from the narrow path that led to a small wooden gate which opened out on to a lonely side lane.

Turning to stroll back to the house, Raine heard a car and, twisting round, she saw Maurice driving slowly along the wide avenue of trees which was the main entrance to the house and gardens. Her eyes lit with pleasure and she found herself hurrying towards the place where she knew he would stop his car.

'Hi, there!' he greeted her as he emerged from his seat after switching off the engine. 'You look like a breath of spring in that white linen dress with those huge red poppies printed all over it!'

She laughed, a joyful tinkling laugh that seemed to carry with it all her dejection, scattering it to the breeze drifting in from the sea.

'This is a pleasant surprise, Maurice. Have you come to see Darius on business?'

'Ostensibly, yes,' was his swift rejoinder as his smile broke. She noted his glance was sweeping her from head to foot, but not in the way of her husband's arrogant examination which invariably seemed to strip her naked. Maurice's eyes were filled with admiration ... and something which, she thought, might even be deeper.

'What do you mean, ostensibly?'

'I wanted to see you,' he told her softly. 'When I was here before you admitted there was a mystery connected with your marriage to Darius; I also gained the impression that you were virtually a prisoner here. In fact, I was just asking you about it when Darius and Marcella returned, and our conversation had to be cut short.' He stopped, watching the gardener as he drew closer. 'Is that fellow listening in to what I'm saying?' he queried in an angry whisper.

'He could be.' Raine, having been treated so badly by her husband, was ready for the balm which she knew Maurice could give her. Yet she was aware of the risk she was taking. If Darius should even begin to suspect there was friendliness existing between her and Maurice, there was no knowing to what lengths his fury would take him.

'It could be?' frowned Maurice, looking sharply at her. 'So you *are* a prisoner?'

'You're very astute, Maurice,' she found herself saying.

'You don't deny it, then?'

'You didn't expect me to, I think?'

He fell silent for a space, his forehead puckered in angry thought.

'Raine—I've got to know what this is all about. I'm going to confide in you something which, in ordinary circumstances, I should never think of divulging.' He glanced around. 'Is there anywhere where we can talk in private?'

'No, I don't think so.' The gardener was still hovering close and, her temper rising, she told him curtly to go and weed the herbaceous border at the other side of the lawn.

He hesitated, his glance shifting to a window at the side of the house—the window of Darius's study.

'I'll ask my master,' said the man after a small hesitation. 'You see, Mrs Darius, he tell me to work here.'

'Here?' Maurice interposed, deliberately pointing to the place where the man was standing, a hoe in his hand.

'Yes, that's right.'

Maurice and Raine exchanged glances.

'In that case,' said Raine, 'you must carry on work-ing here.' And she and Maurice strolled away, to the far side of the lawn.

'Along here,' she suggested, choosing a narrow path between shrubs and trees. 'We'll see what happens.'

'I can't think what can possibly be going on,' said Maurice at once, glancing round to make sure he and Raine were out of sight of anyone. 'Are you really mar-ried to Darius?'

Her eyes widened.

'Of course,' with a hint of anger. 'What do you take me for——?'

'Oh, I didn't mean anything wrong—er—in that way,' he broke in, embarrassed by his previous lack of diplomacy. 'I wondered if he had some sort of hold on you?'

'Only that he's my husband,' was Raine's answer, uttered in flat dejected tones. She was almost on the point of confiding in him totally, and then asking for his help in getting away.

'You must have married him willingly?'

She nodded her head.

'I did, and then we had a—a ...' She could not con-tinue, for as before she was unable to show disloyalty to her husband. It was absurd, but a fact for all that. She shook her head at his prompting glance and said, 'I'm sorry, but I can't tell you everything.'

'I see ...' He did see; she realised this at once. Very perceptive, he was, but anger lurked within him, and indignation as well. These sensations underwent an in-crease when, turning his head on noticing Raine's sud-den frown, he saw the gardener working not too far away.

'I thought you were told to work over there?' Raine spoke sternly, attempting to assume an attitude of authority, but the man, smiling to reveal several bright gold fillings, informed her that his master had told him to work here once the other border was completed. 'And is it completed?' she inquired crisply, and the man nodded his head, again producing an affable smile.

'Yes, Mrs Darius, I have just now finished the weeding. So I come here.'

Maurice's eyes glinted. Raine thought, not without a trace of amusement, that even had she wished to keep secret the fact that she was a prisoner she would not have been able to do so.

'In that case,' he said determinedly, 'your mistress and I will sit over on the other side of the shrubbery.' A pause and then, hardily, 'Make sure you do this border thoroughly, won't you?'

'Of course, Mr Maurice!'

'In which case,' went on Maurice, 'it should take you at least an hour.'

Silence. Maurice and Raine strolled away, but when on reaching the shrubbery they both looked back, it was to see the gardener making for the house.

'He's going to report to Darius,' said Raine unnecessarily.

Maurice nodded frowningly.

'Tell me, quickly, just what is going on?'

'You said you'd confide in me,' she prompted him.

'I did.' But he seemed even now to hesitate. 'It's about my sister,' he said at length.

'You said as much the other evening,' she reminded him gently. He was looking into her face; she noticed a muscle move in his throat, saw the deep admiration in his eyes. She looked at his features, liking what she saw. He was nice, unaffected, no arrogance about him but

134

yet a firmness which she could admire. He was good-looking in a much milder way than Darius, his eyes were kindly, his mouth full and compassionate. Raine suddenly felt like a child who, having been scolded over and over again, longed to be petted and comforted.

'Marcella can't ever have children. That's the reason —so I believe, why she and Darius never married.'

'I see ...' Raine glanced towards the house, expecting her husband to emerge at any moment. 'You believe that, had your sister been able to have children, Darius would have married her?' It seemed feasible, she thought, seeing that they were still excellent friends.

'I do believe that, yes,' was Maurice's frank rejoinder. 'But as things are, Darius would not want to marry a woman who was unable to give him an heir. He's an extremely wealthy man, as you know.' He was looking curiously at her and she knew what was coming even before he spoke. 'Why did you marry him, Raine?'

'It was for revenge,' she admitted after a slight hesitation.

'Revenge?' he echoed. 'For what?'

'That is the part I can't speak about, Maurice.' She glanced apologetically at him. 'It would be disloyal to my husband.'

Maurice's eyes opened wide.

'Do you owe him loyalty, Raine?'

She frowned a little. This conversation was so intimate—just as their conversation had been intimate on that first evening when they had been left together by Darius and his old flame.

'Perhaps I don't owe him loyalty,' she admitted at length. 'But it's a matter of honour—my own conscience, if you know what I mean?'

'Yes, I do, but I wish you would tell me the whole, Raine?'

'It isn't possible.'

'You can't come out with me?'

She shook her head.

'That too is impossible.'

His eyes examined her face searchingly.

'You'd like to?'

She had to be honest.

'I'd love to, Maurice.'

His face was a study of dejection.

'Unless I know everything,' he told her at last, 'I can't help you.'

'Help me?' Her heart gave a leap as hope rose within her. 'What makes you think I would welcome help?'

'It's written in your face that you're unhappy; it must be because you are Darius's prisoner, because there can be no other reason.' He paused a moment, but she did not speak. 'You admitted to there being a mystery attached to your marriage, Raine, and all I can work out for myself is that Darius, having some strong hold over you, forced you into marriage——'

'You asked me just now if I'd married Darius willingly,' she interrupted to remind him, 'and I said that I had done so.'

'Of course. I forgot that.' He paused again, frowning heavily now. 'Do you want to get away from him, Raine?'

She looked down, wondering how the conversation had become so very personal, so very intimate that here was Maurice, who until recently had been a total stranger, offering to get her away from her husband.

Why wasn't she eagerly giving him her answer? What was the strange inexplicable tremor in her heart which she was trying desperately to understand? She wanted to get away from Darius! It was an obsession and had been ever since she had come to Delphi. Maurice was

136

moving impatiently at her side; she looked up into his troubled countenance and said,

'Yes, I do want to get away from him——'

'Quiet!' broke in Maurice warningly. 'He's here!'

They both turned and Raine noticed, with deep admiration, how easily a smile came to Maurice's lips, and how casually he was able to say,

'Ah, there you are, Darius! I was reluctant to disturb you, when I saw you were not about, so I've had a chat with Raine while I was waiting for you to appear. I expect you've been busy in your study?'

Darius nodded his dark head, his eyes never leaving his wife's face. It was flushed, she knew, and her heart was beating so madly that she thought he surely must be able to hear it. She was afraid, terribly afraid that her husband, with his keen perception, would have guessed that some intimate conversation had taken place between her and Maurice. Yet the next moment she was chiding herself for her absurd fears; Darius could not possibly have guessed at the subject of their conversation. It was her guilty conscience only that bred these fears, making her appear culpable, as if she had something to hide.

'Yes, I was rather busy. Was it something important you had to say to me?' He spoke to Maurice, but his eyes had strayed to the other side of the lawn where the gardener was now working again. Raine, her eyes also straying to the man, wondered just what he had said to her husband. Enough to bring Darius out, apparently, which was, of course, exactly what both she and Maurice had expected.

'Well, it's important to me,' answered Maurice. 'I remember your once saying that a friend of yours admired some of my paintings, and I wondered if he'd like to buy one or two.'

'He might,' returned Darius non-committally. 'Is it imperative that you sell your pictures here? I thought you had more than enough customers in England?'

So suave the manner, so impersonally cool the tone of voice. Raine felt again that her husband suspected something.

'I'd like to sell a few here,' said Maurice pleasantly. 'As you know, Marcella and I came into money, but we've been spending—not extravagantly, mind—and it's dwindling rapidly. I can go to England to sell my pictures and come back, of course, but it would be so much simpler if I could get myself a small, select clientele here, in Delphi.'

'I'll see my friend,' promised Darius, and then, gesturing towards the patio, 'You'll stay for some refreshment?'

'Thanks, I'd like a drink of lemonade or something. This heat becomes a bit much by this time of the day.'

Darius saw them seated on rattan chairs, then went off, to get the drinks himself instead of ringing the bell for one of his servants.

'We've got to beat this close watchfulness, Raine.' Maurice spoke swiftly, as soon as Darius was out of earshot. 'I think I know how to do it.'

'You do?' with an eagerness that brought a smile of satisfaction to her companion's lips. 'How?'

'I shall have to use my sister——'

'Marcella? But is that fair?'

'She won't know,' he returned blandly. 'But even if she did she wouldn't mind.' He looked directly at Raine. 'She still thinks a lot of Darius, even though she's resigned to the fact of his having married someone else.'

'How are you going to—er—use her?'

'I haven't quite made up my mind, Raine. All I know

138

is that if Darius is asked to do something for her he'll go out of his way to oblige.'

Raine was silent, aware of a strange oppression and yet quite unable to describe it to herself, or discover its cause. All she knew was that she did not altogether like the idea that Darius would go out of his way to oblige Marcella.

'You'll manage to get into touch with me?'

Maurice nodded.

'I can call here again, on some pretext or other. I used to drop in regularly last year when Marcella and I were staying here in Delphi. We've a house close to the other one—rented of course for the season—so it's no great distance for me to come here, to your house. However,' he added swiftly as he saw Darius coming back, carrying a tray of drinks, 'I'll not be in touch with you until I've made some concrete plans ...' He allowed his voice to fade, managing a thin smile as Darius reached the table and put down the tray. Half an hour later Maurice had left and Darius, still sitting on the flower-bedecked patio with his wife, looked directly at her and said, assuming a deceptively casual tone of voice,

'How long had Maurice been here before I joined you?'

Raine hesitated, hoping she was not as pale as she felt.

'I don't really know, Darius. I don't think of looking at my watch.'

'Are you being sarcastic?' he inquired softly, his dark eyes narrowed and glinting.

'What is the reason for your question?' she wanted to know. 'Your first question, I mean.'

'I was merely interested to know how long you and Maurice had been talking.'

Her eyes wandered to the border which the gardener had been weeding. The man was nowhere to be seen at this moment, but Raine knew for sure that if her husband should leave her he would appear within seconds.

'Why didn't you ask the gardener?' she said at length.

'Because it was my intention to ask you.'

She looked at him, wondering if it were her imagination, or if there really was a challenge in his voice.

'As I've said, I don't know.' Her manner was cold, her tone crisp. 'Does it matter, Darius?'

He said nothing for a moment; she saw that his eyes had wandered to a distant hillside where two black-robed women sat talking, while their goats nibbled at some sparse vegetation close by. The hills looked peaceful against the wild idyllic landscape of the mountain, with the shining rock faces of the Phaedriades reflecting the dazzling sunlight which seemed to accentuate the tranquil grandeur of the whole incredibly beautiful scene.

'I don't suppose it does matter,' came Darius's response at last. 'I was merely interested, that's all.'

She looked swiftly at him, vaguely conscious of a hint of weariness in his voice. He seemed to have decided not to pursue the matter, yet she had the impression that he was still interested in knowing just how long she and Maurice had been together in the garden. His eyes had wandered to the hills again; she watched intently, noticing his glance moving, until it reached the Sanctuary in the distance. The Temple of Apollo stood out, majestic and distinct, impressive monument to a mystic cult long dead, but the spirit remained, and sun-worshippers still came to Delphi, to stand in awe and wonderment before the mighty temple which had been built by the suppliants of the God of Light and Beauty.

Something made Raine say, in a soft and faintly per-

suasive tone which surprised her even more than it surprised her husband,

'I haven't been to the Sanctuary, yet, Darius.'

His eyes shifted, to settle on her lovely face. He
seemed to frown deep down within him, and once more
she gained the impression of weariness. To her astonishment she heard him say,

'When would you like to go, Raine?'

She stared.

'You mean—you'll take me?' She would of course
have much preferred to go with Maurice, but her husband's offer was still most acceptable.

'Why the surprise?' he wanted to know. 'I've taken
you out before.'

'Only when you've been going into Delphi village for
something for yourself. You've then asked if I'd care to
go with you.' She paused, but receiving no comment
she added, 'This would be just for pleasure.'

He looked at her and she noticed the brooding expression that had entered his eyes.

'Then we'll go out for pleasure,' he said, surprising
her once more.

Her feelings were mixed, for although she wanted to
visit the Sanctuary she felt that to go with her husband
would in fact take most of the pleasure out of the trip.
Had she been able to go with Maurice, they would have
chatted together, have commented on various aspects
of the ancient site. Maurice would have explained so
much to her, whereas Darius would in all probability
be morose, as usual, and if he did answer her questions
she would have the impression that his patience was
being tested to the limit. In consequence she would
eventually refrain from asking questions and she and
he would wander about in a tensed, unfriendly silence.

However, she decided to accept his offer and to her

surprise Darius not only seemed willing to answer her questions, but actually became expansive as time went on.

'I don't know if you experience it, Raine, but whenever I come to this place I have the feeling of timelessness, as if I'm in another world altogether, a world where time, as determined by man, does not exist.'

She turned sharply to stare at him in surprise.

'How strange that you should feel like that. I felt it immediately I came on to the site.' She seemed unable to accept that she and her husband had something in common. 'I'd never have believed that you could experience such a feeling.'

A faintly bitter smile curved his mouth.

'You give me credit only for the prosaic, the practical, is that it?'

She hesitated, wondering what to say to this, as she had a strange reluctance to arouse his animosity.

'No, I don't think so,' was her mild rejoinder. 'I just thought, I suppose, that you would be so used to this place that impressions were no longer strong enough to affect your—er—emotions.'

His smile lost its bitterness.

'Being diplomatic, eh? I wonder why?' They were approaching the shrine of Apollo; the ground underfoot was uneven, strewn with broken stones which once had been beautiful marble columns or the bases of statues, and Darius, watching Raine as she walked along, suddenly caught hold of her arm.

'Oh ... thank you,' she gasped. 'I almost fell!'

'Take more care,' he warned. 'You can easily sprain your ankle on ground like this.' His hand was still beneath her elbow; there was an unusual gentleness about his touch that disturbed her profoundly, affecting her senses in a way she failed to understand. 'Why were you being diplomatic, Raine?' he wanted to know. 'After all, it isn't at all like you, is it?'

Again she knew a reluctance to utter any retort that would antagonise him.

'I want to enjoy this trip,' was all she said, knowing he would understand. 'The moonlight on the mountain —isn't it wonderful?'

He looked up at the rock face rising above the temple. Silvered by the glow of a full moon, it was like a gigantic wall of reflected light, mysterious and awe-inspiring, creating a thousand and one images of a world where pagan deities ruled supreme, and where pilgrims worshipped in deep reverence, fearing the wrath of the all-powerful gods of Olympus.

'Yes,' agreed Darius softly. 'It is wonderful, very.'

Raine glanced back, the way they had come. One or two people were walking about, people who had obviously preferred to come late at night rather than in the searing heat of the day.

She stopped, and glanced up at her husband. All was so still and silent over the Sanctuary itself, for the people were some way off. Darius, tall and straight, with clear-cut classical features, seemed all at once to be like a god himself, a god to be looked up to, revered, held in awe. She thought of her first fiancé, and then of Stephen ... and wondered what she had seen in either of them. True, she had never been in love with Stephen, but for all that she had found him reasonably attractive. But now, comparing him with Darius, she admitted to the unqualified superiority of her husband.

Where were these thoughts taking her? Strangely, the one dominating idea and wish that had occupied her mind almost to the exclusion of all else—that of escape—had no place at all in her thoughts at this time.

Darius's voice, soft and inquiring, broke into her reverie as he asked,

'What are you thinking about, Raine?'

'This fantastic place,' she lied. 'Tell me about it, Darius.'

'Let's walk over to the temple first.'

They had come up from the village, passing the sacred Castalian Spring which spumed forth from a deep crack in the rocks, and then strolling along the Sacred Way, following its crooked course which, in antiquity, had been followed by thousands of pilgrims intent on consulting the Oracle or worshipping at the Shrine of the Sun-god, the mighty Apollo, son of Zeus, the king of all the Olympian deities. Lining both sides of the Sacred Way were, in ancient times, the most beautiful statues in ivory, bronze and gold. Darius had explained that the bases now seen had given the archaeologists all the information they needed to tell them about the various statues. The first monument, Darius had said, was that of a bronze bull, dedicated by the people of Corfu about the year 500 B.C. in thanksgiving for a stupendous catch of fish for which—they believed—a bull was responsible. Just a little farther along were the offerings of the Arcadians—nine beautiful bronze statues of gods of Olympus. On the opposite side were thirty-seven statues, offerings of the Spartans in thanksgiving for their glorious victory over the Athenians in the year 404 B.C.

These and many more must have created a most impressive entrance to the sacred shrine itself, the temple towards which Raine and her husband were now strolling, the temple which was the focal point of all the Delphic mysteries, for it was here that the priestess inhaled the vapours through which she was able to speak to the priests.

CHAPTER NINE

RAINE stood in silent wonderment, trying to visualise the Temple of Apollo as it was originally when it had forty-two outside columns of the Doric order. Now there was little left, but the plan was fairly clear.

'It was inside here that the priestess inhaled the vapours which sent her into a trance?' Raine smiled as she spoke to her husband. He nodded, his attention caught by the smile, the spontaneous manner, the pleasant tones she used.

'Yes,' he answered. 'She then babbled strange words to the priests who in turn conveyed these messages to those seeking advice.'

'Even heads of states came for advice, didn't they?'

'Yes, indeed. The Delphic Oracle was respected all over the known world. Delphi itself became a diplomatic centre and, later, a great cultural and athletic meeting ground. It was also the most holy place in the world, and the richest.'

'Because it received so many gifts, of course?'

'Thousands of statues were stolen—five hundred went to Rome alone, and many others to Constantinople.'

'So, in the end, it lost its respect?'

'Everything that is great falls eventually,' answered Darius in quiet, serious tones. 'Delphi finally fell because of the coming of Christianity. Theodosius forbade the worship of Apollo and in so doing literally destroyed classical Greece.' His voice had taken on a note of regret, and as she looked up into his dark forbidding countenance Raine wondered if there was, after all, a little sentiment in his make-up, a little softness in his heart.

'It must have been a most impressive sight when it was in its heyday——' Raine broke off to glance around. 'The treasuries filled with lovely golden ornaments, the thousands of statues . . .' She shook her head. 'My imagination can't stretch far enough,' she laughed.

Darius stared down at her from his great height, his eyes strangely brooding as he said,

'You laughed . . .' And that was all. He fell into a silence which, for some inexplicable reason, Raine dared not break. Within her, something stirred, like the fleeting catch of a dream that was pleasant. She was conscious, for the very first time, of deriving a certain pleasure from his company . . . and conscious also of an access of longing she had never before experienced. She brought back into her memory those times she had enjoyed with her first fiancé, and now she was admitting that they had been by no means as perfect as she had believed them to be.

'Shall we go up to the top of the theatre?' Darius spoke at last, a smile in his eyes. 'I'd better take your hand.'

Without hesitation she placed her hand in his and they ascended the steps, climbing right to the top. Here, away from those few others on the site, they seemed to be alone in the world, just two people in a timeless void, close, but yet with nothing tangible to bind them together. Raine thought of all the wild beauty around her, and felt a loss within her. She knew what it was, but for the moment she was loath to admit it. Her sister would not have felt this loss . . . because she would have been with the man she loved.

Yes, Raine did admit it at last. She would have been

in heaven, here in this magnificent wilderness which was also a paradise of exquisite beauty, if she had been with someone she loved, and who loved her.

Unconsciously she gave a small sigh which was heard by Darius. He stopped and looked at her.

'What was that for?' he wanted to know, at the same time sitting down and pulling her down with him. 'You're not tired?' His tone held a tinge of anxiety and she wondered greatly at the change in him. Was it the Sanctuary which had temporarily mellowed him? Isolated as it was, enveloped in a deep silence and enclosed by mountains and the Sacred Plain of Amphissa with its 'sea of olives' reaching down to the lovely Gulf of Corinth, it seemed to pour out its peacefulness, as if the sleeping gods still wielded their power over man's mental state. 'I said,' repeated Darius, 'what was that for?'

She looked at his profile, strong in the moonlight, yet in some strange unfathomable way, appealing, like that of a child who yearns for something out of reach.

'The sigh, you mean?' she said, playing for time.

'The sigh,' he echoed briefly.

She wondered what he would say were she to tell him the real reason for the sigh.

'I expect it was an automatic thing,' she began, when he interrupted her.

'It was not automatic, Raine.' He turned his head to look at her. 'Why can't you stop prevaricating?'

She frowned at the word.

'What do you mean?'

'You know what I mean. You quite often evade an answer to the questions I ask.'

She bit her lip, and frowned a little as she said,

'Your questions are so pointed, Darius—as if you would probe into my very soul.'

He stared at her, then shrugged his shoulders.

'Perhaps I dislike the idea of your having so many secrets from me, Raine.' No harshness in his voice as he spoke, no animosity or contempt such as he normally betrayed when speaking to her. Again she sensed a weariness about him, a hopelessness even ... But no. Why should she have an impression like that? It was almost as if she were telling herself that he was suffering mentally, but she knew him well enough to be sure that his hardness would be an efficient barricade to any form of mental suffering which might otherwise have assailed him.

'We all have secrets,' she told him softly at last. 'You yourself have many, I expect?'

He nodded then and admitted that this was true.

'Nevertheless,' he added, much to her surprise, 'they are not secrets that I could not share with my wife ... if my wife and I happened to be in love with one another.'

She flashed him a glance, aware of a tingling sensation running along her spine.

'That,' she murmured, aware of a slight huskiness having affected her speech, 'is a most odd thing for you to say.'

'I suppose it is,' he agreed after a moment's consideration. 'Because, of course, there's no love between you and me—nor is there ever likely to be any,' he added, and for no reason at all Raine flinched inwardly.

She turned from him instinctively, conscious of a reluctance to let him see her expression. The visit, which had begun so pleasantly, seemed to have been spoiled by Darius's words, and yet she could not think why this idea should have come to her. What he said made little difference to her; and in any case, he had spoken only the truth when he said there never would be any love between them. Too much had happened even for them to respect one another—on his part the blameworthy conduct at her engagement party, and afterwards, both at the caravan and at the cottage. On her part, the mercenary reason for agreeing to marry him, and the revenge, of course. Yes, she mused, as she sat there, high above the remains of the sacred temple, looking away into the distance where the gorge of the Pleistos opened out on to the sacred Amphissian Plain, far too much that was unsavoury had occurred between her husband and herself that nothing short of a miracle could put right.

It was some time later when Darius suggested they make their way home. She nodded, yet was suddenly filled with an inexplicable reluctance to leave the Sanctuary. For the last couple of hours she and her husband had been in harmony; they had wandered to the top of the amphitheatre hand in hand, almost like lovers, she thought, recalling two recent circumstances, one when she had told herself that she must examine her feelings, and the other when she had known a new and pleasant stirring of her emotions. There had been occasions when she had desired to be intimately close to her husband, when she had had no wish whatsover to resist his passionate lovemaking but instead had responded willingly. She had owned very early in the acquaintance-ship that he possessed the power to stir her, to awake within her a desire for his nearness. And now, when at last he had suggested they leave the silent Sanctuary, with its lonely eagle crags and slumbering pagan gods, she found she wanted only to stay ... for ever if that were possible. Stunned by this admission, which seemed to have infiltrated her mind in swift but gentle stages, she knew without any doubt at all that she was not now anywhere near as obsessed by escape as she was.

'What it is?' Gently came the voice of her husband,

borne on the heady night-scented air. 'You're hesitating.' They were standing by the Athenian Treasury, two figures silhouetted in the moonlight, with all around them the wild primeval beauty, and the atmosphere of a glorious past when the myths and the gods were palpably in residence here, among the heights of Parnassus. 'Can it be that you are not wanting to go back home yet?'

Raine's eyes flew to his, examining his face—for what? She only knew that his voice had been tinged with pleading, as if he were asking her to admit that she would rather stay a little while longer.

'I don't—don't understand you, Darius.' The words came of their own volition, uttered against reluctance. She had coloured slightly, and wondered if he had noticed. The moonlight was brilliant, illuminating the whole Sanctuary and spreading an ardent glow over the ragged heights of the Phaedriades, twin guardians of this hallowed spot. Raine felt sure the light was more than sufficient for him to see that the colour had risen to her cheeks.

He was nodding his head, and a thin smile hovered about his lips. His eyes were brooding, though, and even yet again she had the impression of weariness about him.

'Perhaps,' he admitted surprisingly at length, 'I do not understand myself.'

Again her eyes flew to his. This kind of talk was exceptional, and totally unexpected. Where was her husband's harsh pride, his arrogance, his attitude of superiority?

She said, aware that her only desire at this particular moment was to please him,

'I'd like to stay here for a while, Darius.' For effect, she inserted a questioning note into her voice, as if asking if it were all right with him. She was being very guarded, conscious of the fact that he could change instantly if he thought for one moment that she had heard that pleading in his voice.

'Very well, Raine, we'll stay. Come, sit here, on this fallen column, and I'll tell you some more about the mythology connected with this Sanctuary.'

She found herself smiling up into his face, saw his eyes soften as they had never softened before and wondered again if it was the holy atmosphere of the site which had temporarily mellowed him.

They sat down, suspended between the high cliffs and the sacred plain that swept down to the lovely Bay of Itea in the Gulf of Corinth.

Darius began to talk, telling her of the beginning when the Sanctuary was ruled by Mother Earth.

'Unlike Christians,' he continued, 'the ancient Greeks believed that the earth was the beginning and that all else was created from it. Gaea—who was Mother Earth—had a famous grandson, Zeus, who became the king of all the gods. He wished to establish the very centre of the earth and so sent out one eagle from where the sun rose, and one from where it set. The two eagles met here, and the *omphalos* became the centre of the world as far as the ancient Greeks were concerned.'

Raine was thoughtful for a while after her husband had stopped speaking.

'Of course,' she murmured presently, 'much of the world was undiscovered at that time.'

Darius nodded his head.

'Yes. When we speak of the ancient world it means, of course, the known world.'

'And Delphi was the centre.'

'And the cave of the Oracle was beneath the *omphalos*.'

'That was not the Oracle of Apollo?'

'No, of Gaea. You have to remember that it was at that time a matriarchal society, with men believing that the female was the sole creator of mankind. They did not know that they themselves played any part at all in the act of creation.'

Raine looked amazed.

'They didn't know that when they—they ...?' She tailed off, flushing with embarrassment. Her husband laughed and said bluntly,

'When they mated they had no knowledge that they were contributing to a birth. They truly believed that woman alone was responsible for the population of the earth. Hence the worship of Gaea.'

'But, later, this all underwent a change?'

'Men suddenly caught on to the fact that they were, after all, of some importance. After that the power of the female declined rapidly, with Apollo taking over here, in Delphi, after killing the Python, guardian of Gaea's Oracle.'

Raine considered this for a moment, then said, as if she just had to,

'Women in Greece—and indeed all of the East—became inferior, and stayed that way.'

Darius's eyes flickered strangely.

'Some women here are inferior, but not all.'

She turned, glancing at his strong and classical profile.

'Those friends of whom you once spoke, who are married to English girls—how do they treat them?'

'As equals, Raine, because you see, they married for love.'

Something in the tone of his voice seemed to be a censure, and she became puzzled as to why this should be so. It was almost as if he were making an accusation against her, implying that she ought to have married him for love! What a strange and absurd notion for her to have gained. Yet she was recalling with stark clarity his confident assurance that he would make her love him eventually. Her eyes widened, for it did seem that he had *wanted* her to love him. But if his only interest in her was desire, then this idea became nonsensical in the extreme.

Her thoughts switched, to Marcella, and she recalled her own reaction when Maurice had declared that, should his sister require a favour of Darius, then that favour would in all probability be granted. She, Raine. had been assailed by some emotion ... and now she was finding that the word, jealousy, was intruding into her mind. So stunned was she by this that for a fleeting instant her mind went blank with amazement. Jealousy ... It was incredible! There could be no jealousy without love, and she was very sure she had no love in her heart for the man who was sitting here beside her, his face clearly outlined in the moonlight, his broad shoulders erect, his noble head unmoving as he gazed upwards, towards the summits of the mountain.

Raine stirred restlessly, and with a small sigh of resignation her husband said it really was time they were making their way back home. He rose as he spoke and reached for her hand. She put hers into his, and realised with a sense of shock that she wanted to curl her fingers into his, to move closer as they began to walk, to lift her face in expectancy of a kiss ...

Reaching the villa, they stood outside for a space, listening to the whirring of cicadas in the olive trees. The wind, a mere zephyr, lifted the scents from the flowers and infused them into the balmy night air. Raine breathed deeply, aware of a new and almost joyful feeling of contentment. And when her husband, lifting her face to kiss her lips, indicated that it was time to go inside, she knew no resentment at his proprietorial attitude, but even gave him a smile and said,

'Thank you for a lovely evening, Darius. I was very happy out there.'

'I believe you were,' he returned, and a hint of wonderment edged his voice. 'Yes, my lovely wife, I do believe you were.'

It was a week later that Maurice again called at the villa. He had brought some of his paintings, hoping that Darius would pass them to his friend for perusal.

Raine knew at once that this was merely an excuse for calling, the real reason for his visit being to see her. She was flattered, and ready to receive the friendliness which Maurice would offer, for Darius had been more harsh than ever with her this morning, seeming to have worked himself into a fury as he reminded her, several times, of her perfidy in marrying him for revenge, and for the settlement she had so cleverly got him to sign over to her. His attitude was puzzling in the extreme, simply because, since the evening when they had visited the Sanctuary, his manner with her had often been almost gentle, and she had begun to enjoy a peace and tranquillity which, a short time ago, she would not have believed possible. But now, as she stood opposite to Maurice and examined his young and pleasant features, she wanted nothing more than to get away from Darius and strike up a real friendship with Maurice. She produced a ready smile in response to his, but she was guarded, knowing she would receive the full lash of her husband's tongue should she act in any way which might arouse his displeasure.

'Yes,' he was saying, 'I'll let my friend take a look at these. They're certainly very good.'

'Thanks, Darius. I hope I'm not putting you to too much trouble?'

Darius shook his head.

'No trouble at all, Maurice.' He gestured towards the verandah, where colourful chairs were arranged around a rattan table. 'You'll stay for something to eat?' It was almost lunch time and Maurice said yes, he would like to stay.

'Marcella's gone into Athens for a couple of days,' he added, 'so I'm fending for myself.'

'Gone into Athens—to see the specialist?'

Maurice nodded his head.

'She's had a recurrence of that back trouble, so she decided it would be wise to visit the specialist.'

Watching her husband's face, Raine could not be sure if she saw anxiety there, or if his expression was one of mere interest.

'I'm sorry about that, Maurice. I'll come in and see her when she gets back.'

'Thanks.' Abrupt the tone now, and a swift glance in Raine's direction. She wondered if Darius had noticed this, then decided he had not because, after a few seconds' pause, he excused himself, explaining that he had several important telephone calls to make.

'So we're alone for a short while.' Maurice spoke as soon as Darius was out of earshot. 'I'm sorry, Raine, but I really did try to find a way of helping you to leave here. I knew that Marcella was having to go to Athens, and hoped she would ask Darius to take her there in his car.' He paused a moment, turning his head as if some movement or noise had caught his attention. Raine said, taking the opportunity offered by his silence,

'That was what you meant when you said you would use her?'

'Yes. I felt I could do so without her knowing. I did suggest she ask Darius to take her into Athens, but she said she'd rather get a taxi, seeing that Darius is now married.'

Raine said nothing to this, but she did wonder whether Marcella was intending to drop Darius altogether. It seemed an eternity since the dinner party and Raine's fervent wish that the affair between Marcella and Darius would be renewed.

'So you haven't managed to think of anything?' Raine spoke slowly, and with a feeling of guilt. She wanted to escape, she had told herself only a couple of hours ago, when Darius was subjecting her to one of his vicious verbal onslaughts. This life was sheer hell and she had no intention of resigning herself to it. Maurice had intruded into her thoughts many times, yet now he was here she felt an inexplicable reluctance to talk of the possibility of his helping her to get away from her husband.

'No, I'm afraid not.' Maurice looked at her, making no attempt to conceal his admiration as he allowed his gaze to rest on her lovely face. 'But I shall think of something before very long,' he added presently. 'Meanwhile, I'm going to ask Darius outright if I can take you to the Sanctuary.'

'Darius took me a few nights ago,' she told him, and saw his face fall instantly.

'He did? So you're quite friendly, then?'

She paused at this, considering.

'We're not always having quarrels, if that's what you mean.'

His eyes flickered with uncertainty.

'I don't exactly know what I mean,' he admitted at length. 'Your relationship with Darius puzzles me. I was thinking about it after I left that night of the dinner, and I suppose I reached the conclusion that it wasn't—er—normal.'

She coloured, but said frankly,

'It's quite normal—in many ways, that is.'

'I see.' He looked questioningly at her. 'And yet you want to get away?'

She hesitated, sighing deeply.

'I suppose I do,' she admitted, 'and yet ...'

'Yes?' he prompted swiftly.

'Sometimes it isn't so bad ...' Again she tailed off, frowning at her thoughts. Undoubtedly her husband's power of attraction was strong, and she had already begun to confess, to herself, that he had spoken the truth when he declared that he attracted her just as much as she attracted him. Only yesterday he had said, the light of triumph in his dark eyes,

'Didn't I prophesy that you'd want more than kisses, Raine? And you do, don't you? Deny it if you must, my dear, but those expressive eyes of yours will always give you away.'

'Am I to take it that you've changed your mind about leaving Darius?' Maurice spoke softly, aware that one of the servants was coming out to the verandah with a tray.

'No, I haven't changed my mind.' Raine spoke firmly, aware that if she missed this opportunity, she might never have another.

The servant, Nicoleta, came a little diffidently, scarcely glancing at Raine. It was obvious that she was embarrassed, and Raine felt her temper rise at the idea of servants being aware that Darius was keeping his wife a prisoner. How they must be talking among themselves! Laughing at her, no doubt, with the men probably making lewd remarks about the relationship existing between their master and his English wife.

Nicoleta began to set the table for lunch, taking the silver cutlery from the tray and placing it down; then came the side plates, and the napkins.

Without a word she left; Maurice was frowning heavily but made no comment, much to Raine's relief.

'Raine,' he said after a thoughtful hesitation, 'do you —like me?' His honest eyes were on her face, probingly, as if he sought an answer there.

She nodded immediately.

'Yes, Maurice, I do like you.'

Again he hesitated, and then,

'We could be real friends?'

'I believe so, yes.'

'And, one day, perhaps more?'

'That's in the future, Maurice. For the present, I'm very much married, aren't I?'

He frowned at this and said,

'I wish you'd tell me everything, Raine.'

She bit her lip, one part of her mind positive in its conclusion that she wanted a friendship with Maurice, but the other half reminding her forcibly of the strong attraction which her husband exerted over her. Was she no better than Darius? she asked herself, by no means for the first time. Did physical desire hold so important a place in her life that it could in the end influence her to the extent of her deciding to remain with her husband?

No! The exclamation was silently uttered, but vehement, for all that. Escape was what she wanted, and if Maurice could help her then she was more than willing to accept that help. However, by what he had just said, that help was not to be yet.

'I can't tell you everything,' she found herself saying, after her companion had given a little cough as a reminder that she had not answered his question. 'It's involved, sort of, and in any case, it wouldn't do any good. It's enough that you know that we married without any love whatsoever between us——'

'Darius for desire and you for revenge—at least you said it was for revenge?'

She nodded, flushing a little at his assertion that Darius had married her for desire.

'What makes you think it was desire on my husband's part?' she wanted to know, and Maurice said at once that this was obvious.

'It's only logical,' he added reasonably. 'If he didn't marry you for love, then it must have been for desire.'

She was frowning heavily now, amazed that this conversation had followed the lines that it had. She knew it was wrong to be talking like this to a man she had met only three times, and yet she felt as if she and Maurice had known one another for months. Besides, she was somehow drawn to him, and this being so, she found it easy to confide—to a degree, that was. She knew for sure that she would never confide in him wholly, certainly not to the extent of relating all that had happened since that fateful evening when Darius had walked into that ballroom and decided, almost immediately, that he wanted her for his own.

Darius came from the house and so further conversation was impossible. Maurice's expression revealed regret, while Raine's portrayed no emotion whatsoever, since she knew it were wiser to be guarded when under the searching scrutiny of her husband's eyes, as she now was. She noticed his gaze move from her to Maurice, then to the table, as if his whole attention had been transferred to the thoughts of lunch.

Polite conversation was carried on during the meal, which consisted of red mullet cooked on a charcoal grill, and delicious home-grown vegetables to go with it. Minos, a rosé wine, was served, but Raine did not have any, as most Greek wines were not to her taste. Afterwards, there were fresh figs and whipped cream, then coffee was served on the patio.

Maurice rose at last, thanked Darius for his hospitality, and for the promise that he would let his friend see the paintings, and then left.

For Raine it was an abrupt farewell, but she knew it was necessary under the circumstances. Yet it was most unsatisfactory, as she and Maurice had had a mere few moments in which to talk ... and they had both been very conscious of wanting more time together.

'I must have some freedom!' The cry was out, escaping before she could prevent it. 'This is no life, Darius! I shan't remain a prisoner any longer!'

'No?' with infuriating calm as he sat back in his chair, one hand thrust into the pocket of his light grey jacket. 'How are you to escape, then?' Slow the words, but starkly invidious. 'Could it be that Maurice is willing to assist you?'

Her eyes flew to his, actual fear in their depths.

'I—don't know wh-what you're t-talking about.'

The hint of a sneer touched the hard, cruel mouth.

'Prevaricating even yet again, eh? But you've given yourself away, my girl.' His eyes glinted with wrath. 'You were discussing me with him, weren't you?' Slowly he was rising, and in a sort of panic Raine glanced around, seeking for an avenue of escape. But his vicious fingers were already gripping her arms; she winced, fighting back the tears which filled her eyes. 'What were you telling him?' demanded Darius, his fury still not released, yet it was there, revealed in the low and guttural tone of his voice and in the merciless grip he kept on her arms, a grip which tightened as she was jerked to her feet.

'Nothing,' she cried. 'You're hurting me——'

'I shall hurt you even more if you don't tell me what you and Maurice were saying to one another.'

'We just chatted—about anything and nothing——' She broke off again, crying out as he began to shake her. Her head was jerking back and forth, her teeth pressed together to prevent her biting her tongue. She felt as if her senses would leave her, and she went limp, accepting defeat under his strength, the strength of unleashed anger.

She was crying quietly when at last, his fury spent, he freed her. She leant against the rail of the verandah, supporting her trembling body with her hands; they were behind her, clutching the rail. All around her was nature's beauty—pergolas dripping with violet and orange bougainvillaea, wide sweeping lawns bordered by exotic shubberies, palm trees swaying against the sapphire sky, the hot sun bathing it all with warmth and brightness ... Yes, beauty all round, but in her heart a bitter hatred of the man whose pagan traits had caused her so much suffering. She managed to say, venom in her tone,

'One day you'll pay dear for the way you've treated me! One day my chance will come!' She was shaking all over, and in consequence her words quivered and her mouth twisted convulsively. She closed her eyes, conscious of the weakness enveloping her body, of the haziness of her senses, of the hopelessness in her heart. 'This can't go on indefinitely. It must end—some time, somehow!'

'Somehow!' he jerked, a thread of greyness creeping along the sides of his mouth. 'What do you mean by that?'

Suddenly she laughed, an hysterical, high-pitched laugh that seemed to cause her husband to flinch.

'So you're afraid I might take my own life? You often remind me that I don't know you very well. Shall I tell you something? *You* don't know *me* either! If you did, you'd have no fears of that kind! I'm not so lacking in spirit that I can't face the future—and fight for my freedom!' She was pale and still trembling, but in her tear-filled eyes was a determination which surprised him, a fearlessness which brought the light of admiration to his own eyes.

The crimson colour that had fused his cheeks a few moments ago had vanished, along with his anger. He was now calm, and as unmoving as a statue.

'I apologise,' was his quiet comment. 'I feared, for a moment, that you were threatening to take your own life.'

She looked at him intently.

'You were actually afraid?' she murmured.

He merely looked at her, meeting her gaze and then, still without uttering a word, he turned on his heel and went through the french window, into the cool dimness of the room beyond. Her eyes followed him, puzzled eyes and moist still from her tears. Darius was acting strangely all at once. Could he be suffering from conscience trouble? Was he sorry for what he had done?— for hurting her as he had? She reflected upon the past few days, and on the way they had passed so tranquilly, with scarcely ever a word of dissension having passed between them—until this morning, that was, when, for some inexplicable reason, he had let her have the full lash of his scorn and contempt.

Now, with his cruel action still on his mind, he seemed to have been forced to take himself from her presence, and she wondered where he was now, and whether remorse was holding him in its grip.

'There could be something soft and attractive in his

make-up,' she whispered to herself. 'Often he is gentle ... like a lover who is really in love...'

In love...? She shook her head, thrusting away so absurd a notion. No man who loved his wife would treat her as she had been treated just now ... at least, not unless he were mad with jealousy...

CHAPTER TEN

JEALOUSY. The word repeated itself over and over again in Raine's mind during the following days, and the result was that she began to regard her husband in a new——and faintly exciting light, searching for clues that might reveal his inner emotions. For, if he *were* jealous of Maurice, then he must love her.

Did she want him to love her? So confused was her mind, so mixed her emotions. She recalled how she had felt when, at the Sanctuary, he had for one fleeting moment imagined what it would have been like had she gone there with someone whom she loved, and who loved her.

'If you want to go into the village today I'm willing to take you.' Darius came to her as she lay on the grass, wearing only a bikini. She had a beautiful tan by now, and as Darius spoke his eyes were taking in every lovely line of her body, every delicate curve.

'I'd like that,' she agreed without hesitation. 'I want to visit the museum?' A question, to which he nodded his head, saying that this would be all right with him.

'I expect Maurice has told you about the Charioteer?' he added, a sudden glint in his eye. 'Perhaps he himself would have liked to take you to see it?'

She went a little pale, but retained her composure.

'I *read* about the exhibits in the museum,' she corrected him softly. 'As for Maurice suggesting that he take me, you are wrong on that deduction too.' Rising as she spoke, she was about to reach for her wrap when Darius picked it up and held it for her to put on. His arms came about her and she felt his chin on the top of her head.

'How beautiful you are!' he exclaimed. 'What is this perfume you have on your hair?'

She mentioned the name and he immediately said he would buy her some more.

'I have a fairly large bottle, Darius.'

'From that pimp to whom you were engaged, I suppose?'

'Stephen did buy it for me, yes.' How long ago it was! Yet not more than a couple of months at the most.

'Go and get ready,' he ordered abruptly. 'I haven't all the afternoon to spare.'

She went off to their bedroom, half expecting him to follow her, and watch as she got dressed. However, he remained in his study, coming out just as she appeared in the hall. Raine stopped for a moment to gaze through the open window that ran right along the south side of the hall. Hibiscus bloomed in a riot of colour in the border opposite; poinsettia and allamandas flourished beneath a deliciously fragrant frangipani tree, while high against the clear azure sky the spidery fronds of date palms moved about in the breeze. Aware that her husband was at her side, she turned her head, and an involuntary smile came to her lips. His expression was fixed, and strange. She heard him give a little sigh, and noticed that his eyes had a tired look about them which was by now becoming familiar.

'Are you ready?' His appraising glance swept her from her shining hair to her neatly-sandalled feet. 'You look charming,' he said, the ghost of a smile appearing as she blushed at his flattery. 'Only a girl as beautiful as you could look so perfectly attired in a simple cotton dress. What colour would you call it?' he added. 'Blue or green?'

'Turquoise,' she supplied in low and musical tones. 'It's a sort of cross between the blue and green you mentioned.' She was laughing with her eyes; unexpectedly her husband bent and brushed her lips with his own.

'Come,' he said with a smile. 'We've wasted enough time already.' But his tone belied the abruptness of his words, for it was soft, and edged with a gentleness she had heard only once before, a gentleness which set her thinking now, as it had then.

So strange a mixture he was! She felt somehow that she had not seen either the worst of him or the best. He could be a fiend, she thought, recalling how his pagan ancestors would think nothing of throwing a child over a cliff if it happened to be born deformed. Here at Delphi, the famous maker of fables, Aesop, was flung from a cliff to his death, merely for some small misdemeanour he had committed.

But what of the best in her husband? Raine had witnessed a certain gentleness on occasions; she had several times wondered if he had a softness somewhere within him. She had heard him sigh, as if suffering a measure of dejection. She had seen the weariness in his eyes, as if he were secretly undergoing a mental strain. Perhaps, after all, he was regretting his treatment of her ... perhaps he was gradually coming to care ...

Realising that she was right back at the beginning, she thought again of the impression she had had—that he might be jealous of Maurice. Not that he need be, she thought with a wry grimace. The way she was kept prisoner left no opportunity for her and Maurice to meet, much less do anything which could even remotely cause her husband to be jealous.

The idea persisted despite this, and when, strolling along the main street of the town on their way to the museum, they met Maurice, Raine watched her husband's face closely as Maurice spoke to her, smiling all the while, his eyes admiring, his manner one of friendliness and charm. Darius's face was an unreadable mask, but his manner also was friendly as he asked Maurice about his sister.

'She came home yesterday afternoon,' replied Maurice. 'She's about somewhere—had to visit the hairdressers. I'm meeting her by the trees over there in five minutes' time——' He broke off and flung out a hand. 'She's here now.'

Svelte and confident in a wild silk trouser suit of beige with light green trimmings, Marcella made an impressive figure as she walked towards the place where the three were standing. Was she aware of the turned heads of the tourists strolling about? wondered Raine. If so, she gave not the slightest sign of it. Her smile appeared immediately; it was for Darius, fading down to a mere curve of the well-rouged lips as she eventually turned to greet Raine.

'How are you feeling?' Darius spoke softly, and with an unmistakable hint of concern.

'Fine. I'm not desperately ill, as you know; it's just that, as soon as I feel this pain coming on, I make an effort to see the specialist. The pain's gone now—and the specialist's as puzzled as ever.'

'So long as you're all right,' said Maurice, 'but I do think someone should be able to tell you what's wrong.'

'One day they will, Maurice.' She turned to Raine. 'I expect you know your way everywhere by now?' she smiled. 'When I first came here I spent weeks and weeks exploring.'

Raine, avoiding the eyes of both men, said quietly,

'As a matter of fact I haven't yet had the opportunity of exploring.'

'The busy little housewife?' Marcella gave a laugh

which brought the colour flooding to Raine's cheeks. Like most other people, she hated being ridiculed.

'No such thing,' she returned, managing by some miracle to keep the tremor of fury out of her voice. 'Just the contrary, in fact. I'm a lady of leisure, spending most of my time sunbathing in the garden, swimming in the pool, or reading.'

'And looking pretty for your new husband,' put in Marcella, just as if she had to. Raine looked at Maurice, seeing his discomfiture and feeling sorry for him. Transferring her glance to Darius, she saw a smile of sardonic amusement on his lips, and a sort of challenge in his eyes.

'Are we going into the museum?' she asked crisply. 'You did say, Darius, that you were in a hurry.'

'Haven't you visited the museum already?' asked Marcella in surprise.

'There's not been any time,' from Darius, feeling, thought his wife, that he had better save her the trouble of thinking up some excuse. 'However, we're going there now. Raine's expressed the wish to view our famous antiquities.'

'And very famous they are,' from Maurice. He glanced at his sister. 'What are you thinking of doing, Marcella? I mean—we could have half an hour or so in the museum, couldn't we?'

Raine, under no illusion as to the reason why Maurice should suggest this, sent her husband a surreptitious glance. His mouth had gone tight, as if he were suddenly experiencing anger.

'I'd love that,' agreed Marcella, and instantly moved to Darius's side. 'I'll come with you and Maurice can be with Raine. She'll probably be asking dozens of questions which neither you nor I will have the patience to answer.' She gave her brother one of her

168

dazzling smiles. 'You have the patience of Job and, in addition, you're exceedingly knowledgeable about such things.'

Maurice looked at Darius, and then at Raine. No one spoke and it did seem that an awkward silence would ensue. It was Maurice who eased the situation by saying,

'Why can't we all keep together? There's no law against it,' he added with a laugh.

They went inside the building, but it was soon clear that Marcella had no intention of their all keeping together. She literally dragged Darius over to one side while Raine and Maurice were looking at the Paros marble statue of a young man who, Maurice was explaining, was worshipped as a demi-god by the ancient Greeks. Raine glanced around, saw that her husband did not seem to mind being lured away from her, but at the same time suspected he would keep an eagle eye upon her in case she should have the intrepidity to attempt an escape.

'So we have a few moments on our own.' Maurice was whispering, his mouth close to Raine's ear. 'You look lovely,' he added, and a sigh escaped him. 'I wish we could think of a way to be together sometimes.'

For some reason Raine had no enthusiasm for talking in this way; she was ever conscious of the fact that she owed something to her husband. But what? She was married to Darius, but, under the circumstances, did she really owe him any loyalty?

Confused by feelings that of late had become more and more difficult to understand, she suddenly yearned for peace of mind, for her life to follow a smooth and pleasant path. But with whom? She glanced at Maurice, and still found him attractive. Her glance strayed to her husband; Marcella's arm was tucked cosily into his and her smooth cheek was almost resting against his shoulder. A strange little lump settled in Raine's throat and although she swallowed repeatedly she failed to remove it.

'Shall we go over and join the others?' The suggestion was out before she could prevent it. Maurice looked swiftly at her and frowned.

'You want to?' he asked in surprise. 'I thought you'd welcome this chance of our being on our own?'

She bit her lip, and nodded automatically, scarcely knowing what was the matter with her. Of course she would rather be with Maurice, she told herself. What did she care that Marcella was acting in this possessive manner with Darius?

'I do welcome this chance of being on our own,' she said at length. 'Tell me about the Charioteer,' she invited, 'for it's that which I've really come to see.'

'The wonderful statue was found during excavations by the French in the last decade of the nineteenth century.' They were walking towards it, while Darius and his glamorous companion were talking together in what appeared to be the most intimate manner, for Darius's head was bent, and it did seem that his lips were far too close to those of Marcella. Raine tried to listen to what Maurice was saying, but she could not concentrate. She realised that she was furious at this neglect by her husband. It would serve him right, she thought, if she made a run for it. She might not manage to get away, but she would at least give him a scare. However, with common sense prevailing, she allowed herself to be guided to the magnificent bronze statue where she stood, awed by the sheer unbelievable beauty of the craftsmanship.

'Who did it?' she gasped in wonderment. 'It's ... too perfect for words!'

'Unfortunately the sculptor is unknown.'

'What a shame!' She stood in silence again. 'It's the work of a very great artist, so you'd think the archaeologists would have some idea who might have been responsible for its creation?'

Maurice told her that two artists of the time had been thought of in connection with this most famous statue, one of the most prized in all Greece.

'Pythagoras of Samos could have done it, or it could have been the Athenian sculptor, Critias. However, no one can say for sure because the inscription giving the artist's name has been lost.'

After a while they moved on; Raine occasionally glanced around, to find that Darius and Marcella were never very far away. Darius was keeping his eye on her, and Maurice commented on it, a circumstance which served only to vex her even more.

'I feel like a convict who's been let out of jail for half an hour but is under constant surveillance all the same.'

'It must be awful,' Maurice sympathised. 'He can't keep it up indefinitely.'

'He has up till now.'

'I can understand just how you feel, Raine. And I wish with all my heart I could help you.'

She said nothing, aware that her husband's whole attention was now concentrated on her and Maurice. The dark eyes were narrowed, the sensuous mouth compressed into a thin cruel line. Raine shivered, suddenly afraid of going home with him. His face looked evil; she would have put nothing past him when he was in such a mood as this.

If only she could escape, today, while she was here. She glanced about her, looking for the exits. Her heart raced as she pictured the scene should she decide to make a run for it. She would not get very far, though, and with a terrible sinking feeling in the pit of her stomach she accepted that her situation was hopeless.

'Raine, is something wrong?' Maurice had seen her pallor and his inquiry was tinged with concern. 'You look ill.'

She shook her head.

'I'm all right,' she told him, but the tremor in her voice could not possibly escape him.

'I don't think you are.' His voice was low, his eyes dark with anxiety. 'What is it, Raine dear?'

Her mouth trembled; she turned towards one of the glass display cases, pretending to be absorbed in its contents. For her husband's attention was still upon her, his expression still warning her that she was in for trouble once he got her home.

'I—I——' She broke off, the last of her colour draining from her face. 'Darius ... he's in a fury w-with m-me.'

Maurice turned, but now Darius's attention had been diverted by something his companion was saying to him.

'Why do you say that, Raine?'

She swallowed, endeavouring to throw off her fears, telling herself that she had no real cause for her assumption that Darius was, by his glances, threatening her, or even warning her. She supposed she was by now in such a state of nerves—after being a prisoner for so long—that her imagination was running riot.

'I'm being foolish, I think,' she answered, forcing a weak smile to her lips. 'I'm all right now.'

Maurice looked at her, shaking his head in a little helpless gesture.

'I don't know what to say to comfort you.'

His words were like a soothing balm to her fears and she warmed to him.

'You've been—kind,' she whispered huskily. 'I needed someone like you.'

'Raine,' he said in urgent, imploring tones, 'let me get you away—now!'

Her eyes looked hopelessly into his.

'It's impossible——'

'If it weren't? Would you come?'

She twisted round, saw the transformation on her husband's face as he smiled down at his companion. Never had he looked at his wife like that, thought Raine bitterly. He was obviously still in love with Marcella and although she might not be able to give him an heir, it was clear that he still ought to have married her. Was he regretting his hasty marriage to Raine? Yes, he must be, otherwise he would not have treated her as he had. Maurice was speaking again and Raine came round to face him. He was repeating his question and she answered him without a trace of hesitation,

'Yes, Maurice, I would come!'

'My car's just along the road——'

'It is?' breathlessly, and without a thought beyond the present few moments. 'If you could go first, and open the door, then I could get in and we'd drive away.'

He nodded; she noticed the whiteness of his skin, the tenseness of his expression. Something made her say, even though she knew the words might mean her chance of escape was lost,

'You'd not be able to continue your friendship with Darius. Perhaps you should think twice before helping me.'

Decisively he shook his head.

'I want to help you, Raine. In any case, I shall not want to stay here if you're in England.'

'I'm married,' she just had to point out. 'There could be nothing except friendship between us.'

'I agree to it. You'll be able to get a divorce.'

Yes, there certainly would be a divorce. But did she want to marry Maurice? She liked him and knew she would enjoy his friendship, but could she be sure that this would naturally lead to some deeper feeling? Ironically she recalled her intention of marrying for money. It hadn't worked and all she wanted now was the quiet, simple life. She had had enough turbulence in the last few months to last her for the rest of her days. Yes, she decided, she could marry Maurice, and settle down to a smooth, uncomplicated routine.

Maurice was whispering, giving her instructions. Her ears were alert to every word, but her eyes were on the couple strolling now in front of them. Darius, though, glanced back twice while she watched, and it did strike her that he could have insisted on the four of them keeping together. Still, they were not really very far apart—a few yards, no more. Darius obviously had complete confidence in her inability to escape. Well, she thought with a great surge of satisfaction, he would soon be gnashing his teeth in fury ... if all went well, she accepted as an afterthought.

'Have you got it all firmly fixed in your mind?' Maurice inquired, and she nodded.

'I know exactly what to do,' she said.

Her heart was thudding against her ribs and she wondered if Maurice was feeling the same. Problems flitted through her mind with lightning speed—the matter of money, the actual departure from Greece, the possessions she had left behind at the villa. Many could of course be replaced, but some were items she had had for years, such as small pieces of jewellery she had picked up at various times on the little antique stall at her local market, or old books passed on from her parents. However, she was resigned to these losses, which were infinitesimal in comparison to her precious freedom. Freedom! Never again to be watched, followed wherever she went, confined to a comparatively small space. Freedom to visit her sister, to go shopping on her own, or just to take a stroll along the lane.

'Get ready to make a dash for the door once we're back in the main hall,' Maurice was whispering. 'Shall I suggest we go now?'

She nodded, and whispered,

'Yes. I'll wait one minute only after you've gone.'

'That's right.' He glanced over to where his sister was pointing out something to her companion. 'Isn't it time we were going, Marcella?' he asked, knowing she would refuse.

She turned and a frown marred her lovely face.

'What's the hurry? Darius and I are enjoying ourselves.'

Darius turned then, and his eyes as they met those of his wife were sardonic. He was again trying to humiliate her by giving all his attention to Marcella, and Raine could have laughed as she thought, 'You'll soon have the opportunity of spending *all your time* with her!'

'Well, we'll go and explore another room. But I must go to the car first. I've an idea I've left the door unlocked, and the camera's in the back seat.' He glanced at Raine, and together they went down to the vestibule.

Darius, Raine noticed, not without some amusement, was already disengaging himself from Marcella's possessive hold on his arm, and preparing to follow closely on the heels of his wife and Maurice. Raine stood by a small relief of Pentelic marble, one eye on Maurice as he walked towards the door leading into the street. He had told her to turn right immediately on leaving the small forecourt fronting the museum; his car was a few yards along, but he intended backing up so that he was directly in front of her as she left the forecourt. The door would be open, and he would set the car moving even before she had closed it, he warned.

Darius and Marcella were far too close, decided Raine, wishing she was one of those ultra-calm people who could retain their composure whatever the circumstances. As it was, her heart was thudding, her pulse fluttering about all over the place. She felt almost weak with the uncertainty of the situation, seeing herself dragged back into captivity even before she stepped into the car, seeing the expression on Marcella's face, the guilt and embarrassment on that of her brother ... and the white-hot fury on the pagan features of her husband ...

'The *omphalos*,' she managed, marvelling at the steadiness of her voice. 'Is there an inscription on it, Darius?'

'Let's go and see,' from Marcella, and Raine just stared, unable to believe her luck. She had visualised having to persist for a while, before she could get either of them to suggest having a look.

But would Darius go over there? He did seem to hesitate, and Raine's heart missed several beats as the second of uncertainty seemed to stretch to a full minute or more. However, as Marcella was already moving away Darius followed, after first slanting his wife a glance which was a mingling of taunting amusement and triumph. He was obviously deriving an enormous degree of satisfaction from this blatant neglect of his wife in favour of his former pillow friend. In his imagination Raine could see him actually gloating over what he supposed was his wife's discomfiture; he wanted her to feel inferior, debased, even.

How little he knew what was really going on in her mind!

She watched them move away, then glanced at her watch. It was almost two minutes since Maurice left the building. He would be on tenterhooks by now, believing something had gone wrong. Raine wasted no more time, but turned swiftly and within seconds she had raced past a couple of astonished tourists and was through the door. Swerving to avoid a child, she raced on towards the car standing with its door wide open.

'Right! We're off!' Maurice was exultant, while Raine, every nerve in her body rioting, just leant back after slamming the door and, breathing heavily, tried to relax. 'You did wonderfully well, Raine! Tell me what happened. I became a trifle scared, fearing that Darius suspected something.'

'For once his keen perception failed him,' she said when presently she had her breath back. 'Marcella took him over to the *omphalos* and I made a rush for the door.'

'So far so good.' His eyes went to the mirror. 'He'll not be able to follow us because we've too great a start on him. Where did he leave his car?'

'In the car park—some distance from the museum.' Raine was thinking about Marcella, and her astonishment at what had happened. She would be wanting an explanation from Darius as to why his wife should want to leave him, and in such an unorthodox manner. Darius, searching for some way of discovering his wife's whereabouts, would have no time for explanations——Or would he? Recalling a previous thought she had had, Raine could not now dismiss the idea that her husband was tired of the whole situation, that he regretted having married her and that he would welcome her desertion. All this did not fall in line with the idea that he might have been jealous of Maurice, but Raine was at this moment far too happy to trouble herself with inconsistencies such as those; she was on her way to freedom and not by any stretch of imagination could she see her husband being able to recapture her and drag her back into the bondage she had suffered since that fearful moment when she had entered her pretty little cottage and found him waiting there.

'Are we going to Athens?' she wanted to know, and Maurice said yes, that was his intention.

'I shall make a few detours, though,' he added. 'Not that I think Darius could stop us now, but he might try, by alerting the police from one or two of the villages, in which case we'd be pulled up and questioned.'

'Could they detain us?' she asked fearfully.

'I don't really know, Raine.' He paused in thought, then shook his head. 'They'd have no valid reason to detain us. No, Raine, even if we're pulled up on the mountain road the police couldn't detain us. However, it's much simpler to try to avoid being pulled up, and this can be done by making the detours I've mentioned.' He paused, giving her the opportunity to comment, but she remained silent. 'Oh lord!' he exclaimed, standing on the brakes. 'You'll need your passport!'

'I have it,' she returned swiftly. 'Here, in my handbag.' Always she had feared that Darius would make her give it to him, but apparently the idea had never entered his head. 'I've kept it with me almost all the time.'

'Thank heaven for that,' was Maurice's heartfelt reply. 'For one awful moment I had visions of all our efforts being in vain.'

'Maurice,' said Raine after a while, 'I haven't any idea what to do when we get to Athens.' He was approaching the mountain road, with its numerous hairpin bends, leaving Parnassus behind, and with it the savage grandeur of Apollo's hallowed Sanctuary. 'I have no money.'

'I've a friend who has a yacht. I'm banking on its being at Piraeus. He wrote saying he would be here this week.'

Raine's heart gave a jerk.

'He would be willing to take me to England?'

'I believe he's going to England after leaving Piraeus.'

'You?' she said questioningly. 'You'll be returning to Delphi?'

'Yes, I shall have to.' He stopped and grimaced and she knew his thoughts were with his sister and what she was going to say to him on his return. Then there was Darius; Maurice did not seem too perturbed by the inevitable interview with him. 'I shall stay for a while, Raine, just to settle up my affairs and perhaps do a few more paintings so that I'll have sufficient for an exhibition when I get back to England.' He slanted her a swift glance, then returned his attention to the road, which he was taking at the greatest speed possible under such hazardous conditions. 'Then I'll be home and you and I will sort things out as best we can.' He gave a small sigh before adding, 'You still don't feel like confiding in me, Raine?'

'I'm sorry, but there are certain aspects of this business which I'd rather keep to myself.'

'You must admit that it's vexing for me not to know what has led up to this escape?'

'I'm grateful to you,' she returned sincerely. 'I shall always be grateful, but I can't confide. I will say this, though: I was the victim of Darius's desire, but I've also acted in the most blameworthy manner.'

'By marrying him for revenge?'

'That's right.'

'It rebounded, obviously?'

'Yes, it rebounded, and I suffered for what I'd done. Darius was furious when he learned that I'd married him for revenge.'

'You married him for revenge, but why did *he* marry *you*?'

She shrugged, colouring slightly but experiencing no embarrassment as she replied,

'For desire. Do Greeks ever marry for anything else?'

'Sometimes, Raine. It's said that when a Greek falls in love it's for ever. He'll never even notice another woman, no matter how beautiful she might be.'

Raine said nothing, but she did wonder why these words had gone so deep, making a strong impression on her which not only brought with it a strange uneasiness but also brought back vividly the idea she had entertained—incredible though it was—that Darius was jealous. And it was certainly a truism that there was no jealousy without love.

She shook her head as she would thrust out this unwanted thought. Darius could not possibly love her. He had proved it over and over again by his cruelty, and his arrogant domination over her.

'This yacht,' she murmured, noticing that Maurice was already making a detour, driving off the main mountain road and taking the narrower lane to a village. 'Supposing it isn't at Piraeus?'

'We'll have to think of something else. But I'm pretty sure he'll be there.' He slanted her a glance which was extremely reassuring. 'He'll be there, Raine, so don't worry.'

'I can't help worrying,' she returned apologetically. 'For even if he is there he might not want an extra passenger.'

'He'll welcome you on board the *Mermaid*,' was Maurice's confident rejoinder.

Fortunately the cottage had not been sold, and within a few hours of landing in England Raine was back in residence. Her sister, after having got over her surprise, offered to drive her over to the cottage and on their way they stopped in town to buy a store of provisions.

'I shall never know what to expect next with you,' Drena said. 'What an adventuress you turned out to be!'

Raine laughed, aware that her sister used the word 'adventuress' quite categorically and not to describe a woman who lived by her wits, as the word had come to mean in modern usage.

'I don't want any more adventures, ever,' she said. And then, 'You're a good sport, Drena. You don't ask awkward questions.'

'That's not because I don't want to,' retorted Drena. 'I'm just itching to know it all! However, we won't pursue this just now. Your future's the most important thing at the moment. What have you in mind?' They were in the pretty little sitting-room of the cottage and in spite of the fact that her sister was here, Raine felt an access of fear in her heart, so much so that her eyes kept darting to the window, from where she could see the drive and part of the gate at the end. Trees hid the other part, and she realised that the right-hand gate could be opened without her seeing it. Still, no one could reach the front door without being seen—— 'I asked what you had in mind, Raine,' repeated Drena, interrupting her thoughts. 'Will you get a job?'

'I think,' decided Raine, 'that I shall move to another part of the country.'

Drena looked perceptively at her.

'You think that Darius will come here?'

'Yes, I do.'

'Well, you have a telephone,' Drena reminded her as she rose to leave. 'Use it if you're in trouble at all.'

Two days later Raine had everything ship-shape and was able to relax, both in mind and body, and to think clearly about her future.

But the more she did think about her future the more bleak and pointless it appeared. She supposed the dejection which was slowly possessing her would pass; she would feel much better if only she were divorced from her husband.

Divorced ... No longer to be Darius's wife. Something seemed to turn inside her, something sharp and painful. And the bleakness took on a much darker aspect, as if no light, no joy was to penetrate it, ever.

Restless now, with all idea of relaxing gone, she went outside and paced the garden, her glazed vision unappreciative of the smooth lawn which she had cut a few hours ago, or the old-fashioned roses climbing right up to the landing window above the front door. Nothing seemed attractive any more; she had no pride in possession as she had when first occupying the house. Her thoughts, defying the discipline she would have put upon them, kept bringing her visions of her husband's house and his garden ... and his face ... The pagan face whose harshness had so often instilled fear into her. She gritted her teeth and tried desperately to put the vision from her, but in vain.

'I must get a job,' she told herself, 'and then it will be easy to forget.'

Why should she be so anxious to forget? Surely this freedom was all part of the remembering of her captivity? For how else was she to appreciate her freedom to the full?

A week passed; she was by now expecting a letter from Maurice, and some sort of communication from her husband. Each night she had retired early, locking and bolting every door and window, making sure that if he did appear, Darius would not be able to get into the cottage before she had time to use the telephone. That he would not hesitate to break in she never for one moment doubted, but at least she would have time to call for help.

She had been home for almost a fortnight when the cablegram arrived.

'Darius gravely ill after accident. Act as you wish.
Maurice.'

Raine stared at the paper, her hands trembling. Darius gravely ill? It didn't seem possible, so full of strength he had always seemed. Act as you wish, Maurice had said, and as she re-read this a frown caught her brow. The words had some deeper meaning, but what? Act as *you* wish. Yes, she had it now. Maurice was telling her that although Darius had not asked for her, it was clear that her presence would help him. It also said that as far as Maurice was concerned Raine was free to make a choice: she must go to her husband only if she herself wanted to do so, and not merely from a sense of duty. So much implied in so short a sentence!

There was no doubt in Raine's mind about what she wanted. The fear in her heart was all she needed to tell her that she loved her husband, that should he not recover then her own life would be worth nothing.

Picking up the receiver, she telephoned the airport. There was a flight that very evening.

It was a week later. The doctor had just told Raine that

her husband would live, and that the improvement was due to her presence.

'He had lost the will to live,' said the doctor gravely. 'He was rambling and we discovered that there had been some trouble between him and his wife.' He looked directly at her as he added, 'It was clear that he loved his wife dearly, that he had loved her on sight. It was also clear—or, it appeared clear—that his wife had no love whatsoever for him. In his ramblings we learned that he knew this in the beginning and yet was very confident of winning her love eventually.' He stopped here, then went on to tell Raine everything she already knew. In his delirium Darius had left nothing unsaid. The doctor knew all about that wedding-night flight, after she had married Darius for revenge. 'I gathered that he had been comforting himself—or endeavouring to—by attaching himself at times to a woman with whom he once had an affair.' Again there was a pause before the doctor resumed, in excellent English as before, 'This woman, Mrs Kallergis, means nothing at all to him now; she meant nothing even before he married you.'

'He might have married her had she been able to have children.' So much had been said already that Raine did not hesitate to make this statement. She knew it would go no further.

'This came out in his ramblings also. There never was any suggestion of marriage between them, just as there is no animosity between them now. However, I believe that the lady in question, and her brother, are even now preparing to leave Greece.'

She nodded; having seen Maurice, she knew this to be true. Maurice had been wonderful, understandingly accepting that she loved her husband, that she wanted nothing more than to return to him if he recovered.

The accident, Maurice had told her, had happened on the mountain road. Another car, careering along on the wrong side of the road, had come round a bend and crashed into Darius's car. Ironically, the other driver was unhurt.

The doctor was speaking again, telling her of the further ramblings of her husband. She learned of his determination to punish her for what she had done, yet all the while he was secretly admitting that he himself had been far from blameless.

'Eventually,' continued the doctor, 'he appears to have decided that the life you were both leading could not go on. He had become tired of it. His love for you was still strong and although one part of him wanted to release you, allowing you to return to England, the other part could not bear the parting. It was a wonder you didn't notice this weariness which had come over him, Mrs Kallergis?'

'I did, but I was too stupid to stop and make some attempt to analyse it. On one or two occasions I fancied there might be a hint of jealousy in my husband's behaviour, and although I naturally thought of love in connection with jealousy, I didn't go deeply enough into it.'

'You couldn't be blamed, Mrs Kallergis. The fact of your being kept a close prisoner must have had an adverse effect on your relationship with your husband.'

She nodded, her mind thoughtful as she tried to find other questions which the doctor might be able to answer.

'Did my husband mention, in his ramblings, anything about my leaving him?'

The doctor nodded.

'He got out his car to come after you, then realised it was hopeless. Later, he decided to follow you to England, but again changed his mind. It would seem that he was by this time considering a permanent parting, being fully aware that he could not force you to return to Greece.' The doctor looked at her and she saw the amusement in his eyes. 'After all, he'd have been a very clever man if he could have abducted you twice.'

She coloured at the idea of this man knowing that she had been abducted. But he knew much more, she thought, so it did not really matter.

'I rather think,' she returned with perfect honesty, 'that there would have been no need for him to abduct me.'

'You mean that persuasion would have been fruitful?'

A smile lit her beautiful eyes.

'Yes, certainly persuasion, doctor.'

He looked at her with a depth of understanding.

'We Greeks are apt to use force rather than persuasion, I'm afraid. You English girls don't like it.'

She said nothing to this, knowing full well that Darius would always prefer force to persuasion.

But she was later to realise just how little she knew him.

He came from the hospital a week later, and a few days after that, with all misunderstandings swept away —for they had talked for hours while he was confied to bed—they were in the garden of the villa, Darius's arm about his wife's slender waist. The moon was full, shedding its argent glow over the lovely house, and the grounds surrounding it, and over the sanctuary below and the jagged, eagle heights of Parnassus that guarded it. Palms swayed against a purple sky; cicadas sharpened their wings, the whirring sound they made mingling with the gentle sough of the breeze as it drifted through the foliage of the lovely poinciana trees and jacarandas which formed the backcloth to the shrubbery with its exotic flowers and heady perfumes.

Raine turned in the circle of her husband's arm, lifting her face in the moonlight, seductively inviting his kiss. He readily obliged, and for a long while they stood, close together, in the peace and beauty of their garden.

'What idiots we've both been,' she murmured, by no means for the first time. 'It took a car accident for us to come to our senses about our feelings for each other.'

'Lucky car accident,' was his fervent rejoinder. 'My beloved, I still cannot take it in that you love me.'

'Nor I that you've forgiven me——' She was stopped by his hand over her mouth, a gentle hand whose fingers caressed in loving silence for a space before their owner spoke.

'Please don't talk of forgiveness, Raine. I treated you abominably, not once, but many times. No, my dearest, if anyone should ask forgiveness it is I.'

He had asked it already, but she did not mention this. It was of no importance, because they had forgiven each other without a word being uttered, on that day when she had gone to the hospital and told him that she loved him and wanted to come back.

'I'm glad that the doctor cleared much of it up for us,' he said as they began to stroll on again, towards the fountain with its shady pool, illuminated by subtle lighting set among the plants growing all around its edges. 'I must have been talking for hours!'

'Indeed yes. There didn't seem to be much you'd left unsaid.'

He looked down into her lovely eyes, his expression so tender that although by now she was used to it, she felt a little thrill in the region of her heart.

'How lucky I am,' she whispered, her voice husky

with emotion. 'Is it really true, Darius, or just a beautiful dream from which I must awake?'

He laughed, as he had laughed many times lately, and she thrilled to hear him now, aware that she alone was responsible for his happiness—and in consequence, for her own as well.

'It's no dream, my love,' he assured her. 'Would you have me prove it?'

A quiver of expectancy swept through her whole body.

'Yes—er—no——'

'Too late!' His ardour fanned, he crushed her to him, pressed his lips to hers in a kiss that was as fierce as it was gentle, as dominatingly possessive as it was reverent and tender. 'Is it a dream, my beloved?' he asked in tones of tender amusement when at last he held her from him, his worshipping eyes gazing deeply into hers.

She shook her head, her own eyes dreamy with desire, her beautiful lips parted, and quivering slightly, as if in subtle invitation.

'No,' she whispered huskily, nestling her head against his cool, linen-clad shoulder, 'it isn't a dream. It's a beautiful reality.'

Harlequin Plus

A WORD ABOUT THE AUTHOR

Anne Hampson, one of Harlequin's most prolific writers, is the author of more than thirty Romances and thirty Presents. She holds the distinction of having written the first two Harlequin Presents, in 1973: *Gates of Steel* and *Master of Moonrock*.

Anne is also one of Harlequin's most widely traveled authors, her research taking her to ever new and exotic settings. And wherever she goes she takes copious notes, absorbs all she can about the flora and fauna and becomes completely involved with the people and their customs.

Anne taught school for four years before turning to writing full-time. Her outside interests include collecting antiques, rocks and fossils, and travel is one of her greatest pleasures—but only by ship; like many, she's afraid of flying.

What does she like most? "Sparkling streams, clear starry nights, the breeze on my face. Anything, in fact, that has to do with nature."